Hattie Almira Reed

The Rocky Mountains at Sunset

and other Poems

Hattie Almira Reed

The Rocky Mountains at Sunset
and other Poems

ISBN/EAN: 9783743306097

Manufactured in Europe, USA, Canada, Australia, Japa

Cover: Foto ©Andreas Hilbeck / pixelio.de

Manufactured and distributed by brebook publishing software
(www.brebook.com)

Hattie Almira Reed

The Rocky Mountains at Sunset

THE

ROCKY MOUNTAINS AT SUNSET,

AND

OTHER POEMS.

BY

MRS. HATTIE ALMIRA REED.

———•———

BOSTON:

PUBLISHED BY B. B. RUSSELL, 55 CORNHILL.

SAN FRANCISCO: A. L. BANCROFT & CO.

1873.

TO

MY BELOVED DAUGHTERS,

JOSIE AND LILLIE,

This Work

IS AFFECTIONATELY DEDICATED

BY THEIR MOTHER.

CONTENTS.

THE ROCKY MOUNTAINS,

AND

OTHER POEMS.

THE ROCKY MOUNTAINS AT SUNSET.

SEE how yon sky is draped with gold,
With shining purple and crimson robes,
Mist-like in form, that far upward stream
In the track just traversed by the blazing sun,
Which smiled ere he retired!   And this
Must be the reflex of that smile.
He dimpled the heaven's fair face
Until it shone with thousand wiles;
He crowned the eternal snows with soft, roseate hues;
Or, creeping over them, he left a blood-red glow
On each frozen, glacial brow, which ever
Smileth back to meet his parting glance.
See yon gray peaks, shut in
By massive folding clouds, changing and mysterious!

7

While between their billowy rifts there peep
Long silver belts, all studded with sapphire rays,
Fringed with amber, or the deeper glow
We see reflected on the lake's unrippled bosom
When at night the newly-risen moon
Smiles far down in its shadowy depths.
Along the lines where stretch the lower hills
Blue lights quiver; and the shadows flit
Up from the hollow gray, now flooded with
Prismatic light, engendered by the roll of fleecy
  waves
Along the margin of the heavier mass.
Oh ! could we but prison the changing opal's gleam ;
Catch the coruscating diamond's fire ;
Grasp the sunbeam, and from its gold extract
The finest germ of all its beauty ;
And gather from the glittering moon that looketh
  down
One beam that could, with its transcendent glow,
Outshine all others ;
Pluck the green from the sounding
Ocean's wave; borrow from the stars their splendor,
Mingling the essence of all brightness with
A rainbow, that a token is of God's promise ;

Then cast them forth against the radiant sky, —
Might they not melt like shadowy mist away
Beside the glory that o'erhangs the western gates,
While, perchance, unseen spirits unbar the portals
    grand,
Fold back the glittering drapery that enhanced
The dazzling radiance of the sun, to witness
His triumphant exit and his last good-night?
Oh! can heaven be fairer? Can the golden streets,
All traversed by that immortal throng, whose robes
    of white
May even now sweep down in wavy fold,
And be a portion of that strange glitter;
That hang up before my vision like a veil,
Dimly revealing what glory may be ours,
When, divested of these earthly garments,
We lie down to sleep in everlasting peace, —
Can radiance of that land exceed
This which now dwells upon the heavens,
And glimmers in its massive grandeur o'er the earth,
Which might, perchance, be likened in its beauty
To the jasper sea of God's eternal city,
Where night never falls, nor day?
If if be fairer, will not the soul

Be dumb forevermore, nor dare to lift

The yearning vision up beyond this pale light's glim-
    mer?

O Father! hear thy sorrowing child,

And let this scene majestic fill my soul

With such thoughts of thee, thy tender love and
    care,

That I may walk the earth as one treads a strange
    land,

But ever sees beyond unfading shores,

All girt about with that immortal light

Which falls upon me now with radiance holy.

I pause; for slowly coming o'er the hills

I perceive the twilight hour in sombre vestments clad.

The clouds begin to break, and float away

Into some mysterious realm; while

Darkness stealeth o'er all the earth,

And from out the descending night

Come shades which will not bear

Day's garish light, and which fall upon my spirit

With foreboding gloom 'mid all the viewless things

That are abroad, hiding their presence in the dim
    night.

Methinks I hear the faint rustling

Of their snowy pinion,
And catch the sound of their departing steps
Through the soft wind's murmur.
But I sit as one girt about with a sweet dream;
Which semblance bears to realities strange and dim,
Ever haunting me, of some far-off shore
That I sailed past, and caught faint gleams
Of its immortal brightness ; while, glittering
In its midst, I saw a sea, broad and grand,
Lying underneath a holy light engendered not
By sun nor moon, nor yet of stars,
But was a reflex of that glory that surrounds
The great white throne.   It flooded, too,
The pearly gates that shut me out.
Lo ! I sailed past into the shadowy world
Beyond ; but, while I wander 'mid its clouds,
I still behold such token of my Father's splendor,
That my rapt soul will evermore retain
The radiant vision, and, through
And through all the years to come, will deem
It but a type of that glory which no mortal eye
    beholds,
But which awaits us on yon deathless shore.

EARTH.

WITHIN the bosom of old Mother Earth from whence
 we sprung,
Where Promethean heats generate, and melt
The massive rocks into a molten glow
Like one vast crucible, resolving the elements into
 form;
Upheaving mountains, from whence volcanic fires
Belch forth, and pour their dreadful floods
Adown the plains in one continuous stream,
Sending sulphuric vapor out upon the air,
And smoky clouds up to the sunlit heavens;
Whose awful voice thunders far above the ocean's
 roar,
When tempestuous winds into fury lash the waves
That coruscate and gleam with lights reflected
From varied forms and hues prismatic;
In voluted caverns, whose labyrinths wind
Underneath, — the mountains lift and bend

To unknown regions, where calcareous pendants hang,
Wearing shape and form no art can imitate;
And stalagmite, presenting to the eye figures
Clothed with the aspect of humanity,
Which ever keep a seeming watch,
Like sentinels frozen into everlasting silence.
Here deep, still lakes repose, unrippled, cold, and
    limpid,
Which, perchance, are fed by crystal drops
Of melted snow, that slip slowly through
Creviced granite and jurassic beds;
And the rivers underground, that swiftly sweep,
Terminating in boiling caldrons, whose rumblings
    low
We hear, like the distant thunder's mutterings;
The eternal mountains, that hang above the hills
In vastness and sublimity,
From which the out-cropping gold is garnered,
Or carried by the ever-changing currents down
Through rugged gorges, overleaping cliffs,
Resting in the huge bowlder's niche,
Or buried 'neath the yellow sandstones, where
Deciduous leaves and earth cretaceous shall hide it,
Until some exploring mind, drawn thither

By magnetic power, shall disembowel it
From its resting-place;
And buried 'neath the crust and mould
That germinate the tiny seeds, from which
Unnumbered blossoms spring to life;
And mighty forests, intwining their gnarled roots
Round igneous rocks, reaching down through soft
Beds of marl and earth erosive, feeding off the sili-
cious mass,
And drawing sustenance from deposits that roll
Down the mountain-side, and are formed
By atmospheric influence into soil alluvial.
Underneath granitic beds drops of carbon
Are resolved into adamantine hardness,
And repose through all the silent ages,
Until Nature, as if wearied of her hidden jewel,
Disgorges it in some convulsive moment,
Leaving it uncovered on the gleaming sands,
Over which clear, limpid waters flow, until
The placer-miner plucks it from its shining bed,
Barters it in traffic, when it is borne
From land to land, cut and fashioned,
And girt about with golden bands, which,
Perchance, may deck the brow of monarch.

O Earth! thou dost bear within thy bosom
Secrets which no eye can penetrate,
No mind can comprehend.   What beauty
Rests beneath thy fertile soil,
Whose blossoming flowers perfume the air,
Whose surface teems with life and joy!
What sublimity! what power!   The hand
That rolls back from the ancient mountain's brow
Its enshrouding mysteries, and bids
The leaping water carry on its breast
Each herald of its greatness, upheaving
From old Ocean's bed the sounding shells;
And gives power to the coral insect, — power
To rear its palace within the watery caves;
And keeps the sun to its appointed course,
And the stars in the vast illimitable dome above us, —
None can comprehend its workings, until, perchance,
Death shall draw aside the veil, and the spirit,
Purified from earthly dross and pain,
Heaven's nearer glories shall behold.

THE SPECTRE HAND.

SEE this lily pale, this lily fair,
All girt about with beauties rare!
I plucked it from yon vale, just where,

Beneath the shade, the winding stream
Reflects in its depths a stray moonbeam;
And glitters there, too, a starry gleam.

On this gemmed couch the lily lay,
So fair and sweet, it seemed to say,
"I bloom for night, and not for day."

Embossed with gold, embossed with green,
Oh! never fairer sight was seen
Than this lily asleep in its velvet sheen.

On swept the waves with musical plaint
Past the spot, where, like some sweet saint,
It lay inwrapped with odors faint.

Slow sailed the moon far above ;
Yet it seemed to look down with eyes of love,
Veiled in clouds like a white-winged dove.

Thou wert like a ghost, O lily pale !
Rising from out the fragrant vale
Where the waves keep up a plaintive wail.

For when over the moon there drifted a cloud,
Misty and white like a spotless shroud,
And the wind found voice to shriek aloud,

O'er thy waxen petals there hovered a hand,
On shadowy finger there circled a band, —
A golden hoop on the shadowy hand.

On a dimpled finger that ring I placed
In years agone, while I fondly traced
The blush that mantled thy modest face.

A jewel it bore of rarest mould,
Like a lily fashioned in bed of gold,
Encircled all with opaline fold.

2

Above this lily there gleamed to-night
On the spectre hand so wan and white
That jewel rare in its glistening light.

What dost thou here, O spirit pale?
Why hauntest thou this fragrant vale
Where the waves sweep by in plaintive wail?

I left thee asleep where the daisies bloom,
To wander afar in despair and gloom:
Why comest thou up from thy lowly tomb?—

Where spring the fragrant grasses;
    Where the river flows;
Where, in shining masses,
    Blooms the pale primrose;
And the purple dasies
    Are nodding in the breeze;
And the freckled lilies
    Droop their emerald leaves
In the limpid water;
    And the bindweed weaves
Around the wooded altar,
    And to the willow cleaves;

While the clouds of gold,
   Flushing all the heavens,
Hang down in massive fold
   Before the gates of even,
Barring from our view
   The pearly streets, the jasper,
The city ever new, —
   Flying ever faster
Across the bending blue,
   Until the solemn Night
Cometh down the mountain,
   And with her shadowy light
Veileth tree and fountain.

Art come from city whose walls are bound
With jasper and pearl, and girt around
With immortal light, and glory crowned?

Ah, sweet soul! come not here.
I saw thee lie on thy sable bier,
Cold and dead, yet shed no tear:

For I pictured thy soul in its upward flight;
And the gates that shut thee from my sight
Oped, methought, into worlds of light,

Where lies a silver sea,
 Placid, broad, and grand,
Begirt by emerald shore,
 Begirt by emerald strand, —
A city with twelve gates:
 The gates are wrought around
With sapphire and with pearl,
 With amethyst all crowned.

Why comest thou from that world of bliss,
In spectre form, to the shades of this?
Findest thou aught up there amiss?

See! the moon is hid in cloudy white:
Oh! plume thy pinions for backward flight;
Retire, sweet shade, to yon realms of light.

For loud moans the wave;
 The wind moans aloud:
Across the moon's disk
 There lieth a white cloud.
I have plucked the pale lily: .
 To me it is a token
Of the hand that bound us,
 Death left unbroken;

For, reaching far from heaven,
 I discern a spirit-hand
Through the gates of even, —
 The invisible band
That will our souls unite
 In yonder deathless land.

QUICKSANDS.

JUST where the surf foams on the pebbly shore
 When the surging tide rolls in ;
And through a chasm by tempests rent,
 Where it beats with unceasing din
'Gainst rocky sides, all hollowed out
With the whirlpool's rush and eddying rout, —

Here the treacherous quicksands sleep
 Like shining grains of yellow gold ;
And bars of white sunshine all softly creep
 Across the gray and lonely wold
That is swept by winds and tidal-waves,
Which come, perchance, from ocean-caves.

And these glittering sands slowly ingulf,
  Their treacherous beauty 'neath,
The unwary footsteps that venture on,
  And mercilessly round them wreathe;
Drawing them down in their pitiless deeps,
Creeping o'er them in pitiless heaps.

And thus in life. I one day roamed
  'Neath summer suns and summer skies,
That aspect wore almost as fair
  As the golden streets of paradise:
And the quicksands of life so smiling lay,
All robed with glamour that happy day,

That with faltering step I ventured nigh,
  Lured by the evanescent light
Which beamed on me, as stars that shine
  On the ocean's bed at night;
But all that was prized the most by me
They slowly ingulfed with mocking glee.

DOWN IN THE VALLEY.

Down in the valley where the swift waters flow ;
Down in the valley where the wild roses blow ;
Where the moon is rising like a fair young queen,
Flecking all the woodland with her silvery sheen ;

Down in the valley, where the night-winds at play
Rustle all the fern-leaves, like fairy-feet astray ;
Where the singing water leapeth all the night
O'er the yellow sands, a band of liquid light, —

Ellen lies asleep : around her form of grace
A snowy shroud inwrappeth ; around her marble face
A rosebud-wreath intwineth ; on her pulseless breast
The folded hands are lying in one unbroken rest.

Upon the heavens I gaze.   One blazing star
Shoots from its orbit into unbroken space afar ;
A cloud veils the moon ; the brightness of the night
Wan shades ingulf ; but a belt of starry light

Crowns all the heavens. Methinks Ellen dwells
Behind that radiant splendor that nightly swells
Into floods of glory up in worlds of light,
Placid, grand, serene, beyond mortal sight.

A MESSAGE.

On snowy pinions, sweet dove,
   Fly afar for me
The swelling tide above
   Of yonder restless sea.

Float not near the cloud
   That crimson hangeth down,
Flaunting its banner proud,
   Wreathed with purple crown.

'Twould robe thee in its fold,
   O bird of snowy wing!
Soaring through the misty gold
   That round the sunbeams cling.

Fly, swift, sweet dove, oh! fly
   To yonder sunny land.
Around thy tiny throat I'll tie
   A sheeny silken band:
Amid its folds shall lie
   Of hair a yellow strand.

This token bear, sweet dove,
   Swift as the morning star
Dims in the heavens above:
   Oh, fly thou afar

Unto a summer land, O bird!
   Girt by tropic blooms,
Where pale shades and weird
   Sleep in the cavern's gloom.

Pause not in the midnight hour
   Beneath the glimmering moon,
Pale with mysterious power:
   But thy white pinions plume

For the ancient land, the golden,
   Bound by the silver tide;
While the happy hours, the olden,
   Softly forth do glide

From a chamber silent and dim,
    From deathless memory's hall,
Like harmonies creeping in
    That on my spirit fall.

. Then away, sweet bird ! fly away
    Where one awaiteth me,
In the mystic glamour of a day,
    Over the restless sea.

THE DAY IS BRIGHT.

THE day is bright.   I'll gang to the hills ;
    I'll gang to the mossy glen,
Where saft and sweet the dancin' rills
    Are singin' a song I ken.

The loch is shinin' lik' yellow gold ;
    The hedges are bright and gay ;
The purple heather shines on the wold,
    The sun on the fields o' May.

Oh! sair is my heart; mine eyne are dim
   Wi' weepin' in the nicht,
When the mune is pale 'round her golden rim,
   And the stars in the heavens, sae bricht,

Twinkle and twinkle. Oh, my luve is dead!
   And saft the nicht-winds blow;
The wild rose scatters its blooms o' red,
   The hawthorn its blooms o' snow.

But I'll dry mine eyne; for the day is bright,
   And the sun shines sweet and fair:
I'll take my way alang fields sae light,
   Though my heart wi' grief is sair.

Alang the lane where the buds o' spring
   Are breakin' into bloom,
Alang the lane where the mavis sings
   All in the golden noon,

I'll gither from the hedges the blooms sae bright,
   White as the driftin' snow:
I'll scatter them saft, I'll scatter them licht,
   Where my luve is lyin' low.

D E A D.

I'VE been dead these many years:
　　Over me go the wheels
　　In wild discordant peals;
The clanging bells ring out;
And the noisy children shout
　　Merrily across the fields.
Round and round the raven flies,
Dashing up to the bending skies;
　　Then, flapping his wings, away he floats,
　　Croaking forth his dismal notes.
Over my head, by the mossy stone,
The seeds expand by the wayside sown,
　　And bud and break into curious bloom;
　　While up I reach from my mouldy tomb
With icy hand, their roots to twine
Around this marble brow o' mine.
　　Over me go the wheels;
　　And through the sunny fields

The speckled humming-bird
Dreamily floateth, unheard
    By all but me in my mouldy bed;
    While harsh and discordant over my head
The wild and·clanging bell
Pealeth forth a dismal knell.

In years agone I shut my eyes
    To dream an hour away
 ` Until the drowsy Day
Should don her nightly robe,
And all upon the globe
    Be wrapped in blessed sleep;
    While the stars above, that keep
Their evening lamps a-trim,
Faintly burned, and dim.
    I awake beneath this mould:
    Round and round in icy fold
Death inwraps me; and the wheels
Crunching go over the fields.
The gold of my hair intwines my feet:
    No lady in her bower,
    Dreaming by the hour,
Hath such silken sheen
In her locks, I ween.

Seeming I lie asleep;
But I wake, and weep
That over me go the wheels,
And the clanging peals,
And the dismal knell
Of a discordant bell.

They bound me with a silken shroud,
And folded o'er my breast
My hands in quiet rest.
With the lilies waxen white,
And roses rare and bright,
They intwined my brow,
Resolved to ashes now, —
All but one tiny pearl
Left in my golden curl:
My bridal veil, like a misty cloud,
Hath melted as cloud away
Afar in the field of day.
Over me go the wheels;
And through the summer fields
The raven circles round;
While dismally doth sound
The flapping of his wings,
And the bell that rings.

There are footsteps overhead
Passing with their heavy tread;
   There are voices faint and sweet
   Mingled with the sounding feet.
Oh ! pass light, pass slow;
And let your music flow
   Like the voice of saint away
   In the realms of endless day.

  There's one I left in years agone,
When I closed my eyes to dream :
Oh! he doth weep, I ween,
   That round and round the mould
   Creepeth like a fold
Over my feet and hands ;
Over the shining strands,
   The silken gold, o' my hair ;
   Around the robe I wear.
Between us lies a yawning gulf
   Spanned by icy bridge,
   Begirt by icy hedge :
Its waves are cold and dark ;
And the fainting traveller marks
   Their chilling, awful swell
   As he glanceth back to tell

Where the breakers loom ahead,
Sweeping round their rocky bed;
　　But all go down in the whirling tide, —
　　Down in the deep, and there abide.

Dead, dead, these many years!
　　Over me go the wheels,
　　Harrowing all the fields.
Hark! the bells ring out;
Merrily the children shout;
　　With heavy tread and slow,
　　Over me come and go
The grating sounds of many feet,
Mingled with the voices sweet.
　　One step falters in its tread
　　As it passes nigh my bed.
There's a rattling sound; a grave yawns wide;
A coffin's lowered close by my side.
　　Now over us go the wheels;
　　The tolling bell in mournful peals
　　Floats far above the withered fields.

THE LOST CHILDREN.

THE warld was still; the mune hung low
   All 'gainst the western walls;
And swift the f'ashin' waters flowed
   Abune the windy falls,

Where lay the snaw so white and braw,
   Lik' a spotless windin'-sheet;
And gleamin' it lay wi'out a flaw
   Upon the mountains steep,

Abune the cot where twa infants lay
   Lik' lambkins fast asleep,
Or lik' twin rosebuds that in May
   Abune the hedges peep,

Wi' folded hands and folded feet,
   Wi' ringlets lik' the gold
That in the mountain-daisies sleep,
   Or 'mong the lilies fold.

3

The nicht was cauld; the winds blew on;
    The stars they blinked sae bricht!
The mune, that shone the hills upon,
    Now bade the warld good-night.

The babes slept on, nae circlin' arm
    Of mither foldin' round
The limbs o' grace; yet each cherub face
    Wi' cherub smile was bound.

The lips were white, the lips were cauld,
    And ne'er would babble more
Beside the waves that slush and fauld
    Around Loch Lomond's shore.

The morn woke up; the sun rose high;
    The warld was on its feet;
The cauld winds blew, and whistled nigh
    The infants in their sleep,

But waked them nae. Oh! sweet the twa
    Must slumber in the cot:
For father's call they answer nae
    Nor mither's croon sae saft;

For a' in the nicht the angels bricht,
    That dwell abune the skies,
Gaed softly by in robes o' white,
    And closed the babies' eyes.

And when the mune gaed quickly down
    On ither warlds to shine,
And the stars that blinked sae braw upon
    The snaws of winter-time, —

All in the dark their sinless souls
    Crossed to the ither side;
And the angels bright in robes o' white
    Carried them over the tide.

LINES ON THE DEATH OF MRS. DE SOTO, BURNED SEPT. 3, 1872.

TOLL, bells! a soul has passed away;
    Pray, priest, in stole of gray,
    Above the casket where the roses lay,

Above their waxen white.
Lift not the lid ; for mortal sight
Will start aghast in pale affright

At the headless trunk which therein lies,
Charred and blackened, with awful guise :
'Tis all that will greet the tear-dimmed eyes.

There's no silken hair to softly fold
Back from the brow in rippling gold,
Or bind or braid, as in days of old,

With a rose that's white, or rose that's red,
And pearl that's rare from the ocean's bed,
Or violets sweet by dewdrops fed ;

No feet to fold ; no hands to lay
O'er her pulseless breast, and softly say,
"She seems asleep this sunny day."

Oh, nought but this ! The roses pale
Lie light upon her, a fragrant veil,
That stilleth never the sobbing wail

Heard in the chancel, heard in the aisle,
Where sweet music stealeth all the while,
As if angels sang in that sunbeam's smile

That lieth on casket, that lieth on pall,
And on her grave will evermore fall
With the tender grace that gladdens all.

O souls that grieve for this one gone!
See ye not her 'midst the shining throng,
'Mid ranks that sing one endless song?

Hear ye not through the clouds the sound
Of angel-harps that echo round
The gates of gold with jasper crowned?

Know ye not now on golden shore
Her feet will falter, ah! never more,
That oft were weary, and bruisèd sore,

As they pressed the flower, or pressed the thorn,
Or meekly waited for the day to dawn
Which ushered in one endless morn?

JEANIE.

O MITHER ! me heart is verra sair ;
  But I'll don me bravest gown,
I'll snood me silken hair,   .
  And gae to yonder town.

Snaw-white and braw shall be the rose
  I'll gither by the way ;
Snaw-white and braw the lily blows
  Where the yorlin croons his lay.

The mavis is singin' in the glen
  Where Jeanie used to sing, —
Jeanie, that died o' grief, ye ken,
  Alang the blooms o' spring, —

Jeanie that was like the lilies' snaw,
  Wi' a rose o' red on ither cheek, —
Jeanie, that stately was, and braw,
  But meek as vi'lets meek.

Jeanie lo'ed : but Jamie was fause, —
    Fause as the fickle wind ;
Cauld winter's blast, and winter's frost,
    Ne'er showin' so unkind.

So Jeanie wilted as flowerets wilt
    Alang the emerant lane :
She ca'ed for her kirtle, she ca'ed for her kilt ;
    And Jeanie's soul was gane.

Now, mither, ye ken why me heart is sair ;
    But I'll don me bravest gown,
Wi' silken snood I'll bind me hair,
    And gae to yonder town.

Snaw-white and braw shall be the rose
    I'll gither in the lane,
Since snaw-white and braw the lily blows
    Where Jeanie's soul is gane.

THE SEA.

THE sea, the never-resting, solemn sea,
   . That rolls in majesty away,
While over countless treasures of untold wealth
    Its foam-crested billows play !

Against rock-bound coast and sandy shore
    The sullen tide rolls in and out ;
And the wild winds sing an anthem too,
    As they restlessly roam about.

When night descends with gentle grace
    Over earth and sea and sky,
And soft stars glitter and shine,
    And the round full moon sails by, —

Then the sea is decked in its fairest robes,
    And its waves opalescent flow,
And gleam with hues of sapphire and gold
    And the moonlight's radiant glow.

And the sea ever remorselessly rolls
    O'er the dead in their silent sleep,
And ever will roll, and remorslessly roll,
    And around them softly creep,

Till the trump of God shall call them up
    From all the earth and lonely sea,
And bid them rise, where from death and sea
    The longing soul is forever free.

BEAUTIFUL TRESS.

BEAUTIFUL tress, that shines like gold!
    Beautiful tress!
    The head you deck,
    The marbled neck
That your glittering sheen infolds,
    The brow you kiss
    With soft caress,
    Each yellow mesh
That downward floats like silken strands
Where folded rest the dimpled hands, —

Beautiful tress on brow of snow!
Beautiful tress!
When sorrow comes,
Will you whiten then
In time's silent ebb and silent flow?
As the years flit by,
Will their echoing sigh
Reverberating die
In Memory's untenanted halls,
Soundless, save when the spirit calls?

MORNING.

Morn creeps o'er the world with silent step,
Trailing her robes of glittering white
O'er these ancient hills and ancient plains;
While the mountains gleam with purple light,
And grandly tower to the glowing skies,
And stretch away in power and might
Each awful chain and dark ravine,

Where the foaming waters madly leap,
And ever rush on with sullen roar
Through rocky caves, where the echoes sleep,
Winding and creeping, with forces spent,
To the lake below, so dark and deep,
O'er whose slumberous waves and soundless shore
No glorious sunlight will softly creep.
But the snow-white pigeon, that rears its young
On the mountain's loftiest peak,
Sees mirrored down in its quiet depths
Its own spotted wing and crimson beak.
When the noonday sun gilds all the earth
With its radiant golden glow;
And snow-crystals melt 'neath its burning gaze,
And softly glide down to the vales below,
Leaving behind them such marvellous blooms
As spring to life by the glittering snow, —
Then, down in the deep and shadowy lake,
Wild, rocky cliffs reflected gleam,
And rifting clouds float lightly o'er;
While all the glory and glint and sheen
That infolds the earth, and infolds the sky,
A soft grace lends to the gorgeous scene.
And, through all the dim ages yet to come,

These hoary mountains will ever rise,
Till time into eternity shall sweep
All that here gather, — the old and wise,
All mourning souls, and those that yearn
For the pearly streets of paradise.

A POEM.

THE poor actor on the stage of life
Frets out his feeble existence in an hour,
And passes on beyond the gates of death,
Where all the rich, the gay, the honored,
The old, the young, have laid down in silent rest.
But the soul, that germ of immortality,
God-given, a part of God himself, —
Where, or in what silent shades, does it repose?
In this fevered life it ever groped in darkness;
Ever with unsatisfied longings upward gazed,
Looking to the light that shines from Calvary's cross.
Oh! could we but peer beyond those realms
Where dwell in holy peace countless numbers

Of souls redeemed, no backward gaze,
No thought of death or pain or parting,
Could mar the spirit's calm :
For on the vision then would burst the light
From golden streets and sapphire walls ;
And on the ear would fall the sweetest music
From angel-harps and angel-voices, ever tuned
To praise around the great white throne,
And by the jasper sea of God's eternal city.
O fair, green earth, with radiant beauty robed !
O still firmament, where yonder stars
Glitter and shine, and where the white moon
Sails on 'mid cloud all silver-tipped and fleecy !
O mountains, that rear your snow-capped crests
To kiss the clouds ! O mighty ocean,
Freighted with costly ships and precious lives ! —
Ye all, all, will pass away, and from your ruins
Rise heavens new, and a bright, new earth.
But the little child who smiles and weeps,
And is so frail that a rude blast
May quench its feeble life, possesses that immortal
   germ
Over which death hath no power.
I pause in silent awe, and ponder

O'er this great plan.
All fame, all pleasure, so little seem,
So brief, so insignificant,
That I wonder why we weep and moan
O'er such little pains and little griefs.
But turn our vision to the blessed light
Which at every toilsome step may brighter gleam
Into the darkened soul; and, as Death approaches
With cold and clammy touch to crush out the life
Of those who walk with us this earthly vale,
It may go with us even down to the dark tomb,
Which ever yawning stands with open arms,
Ready to receive our mortal part.

UNDER THE SNOW.

UNDER the snow she lies asleep, —
Under the snow:
The wild winds blow,
And around her creep,
And around her sweep,
As they come and go.

Her folded hands lie still
    Over pulseless breast
    Forever at rest,
And meekly folded, and meekly crossed;
While I weep for all that I have lost,
    All I loved best.
Under the snow my darling lies cold,
    Never to know
    How I weep in my woe
That the dampness and mould
Her grace doth infold
    Under the snow;
And the stars shine soft and clear
    In the azure depths above
    Like harbingers of love;
And the pale moon sails on,
While a cloud has come and gone
    Like a white-winged dove.
But, if under the snow her form lies cold,
    Under the snow,
    Her soul, I know,
Is dazed by the splendor that greets her sight
With its glimmer and glory and shining light,
    And radiant glow.

PEACE.

ONE day I idly wandered forth :
My soul was wrapped in mournful gloom ;
And all the fair, sweet earth and sky,
And all its blush and all its bloom,
Seemed to exhale a melancholy light,
Faint and dim as shadowy night.
Yet summer airs around me played,
Summer flowers around me bloomed,
And sunshine gilded all the earth :
But it seemed to me like the yawning tomb
That mercilessly swept from my yearning gaze
The cherished friend of other days ;
And I said, " O glad earth and radiant sky !
O summer winds, that sweep
Through waving trees and forests old,
Rippling the lakelets deep !
O blossoming flowers in odorous vales,
And sunshine that leaves a brightening trail,

And bird that sings and circles high,
And sparkling river that rushes by !
In your influence sweet is there no balm,
In your sacred whispers no sacred calm,
My spirit's fierce fear to softly quench,
And bid me look upward, from ever whence
There cometh a light,
Born not of day, nor yet of night ? "
And answer came to my longing soul,
So faint at-first I listed not ;
But truly and gradually around me stole
A light from heaven, or I never knew what :
It might have been a loved one hovering nigh,
Or the glory and sheen of the upper sky ;
But before my vision a form appeared,
All draped in robes that shone
With radiant splendor, and girt about
With such beauty as mortals had never known :
It was white-winged Peace, and her whispers roll
With power and might into my soul.

4

MEDITATION.

OVER heart and over brain how Memory holds her
  sway,
  While through night's solemn stillness no sound
    doth come!
Heavy silence broods o'er mountain, hill, and plain:
  The breeze has ceased its murmuring through the
    leafy dome.

O friends of my youth! O friends of my later years!
  Do you walk the upper plains in the light of God's
    love,
Clad in robes of immortality, so spotless and so pure,
  Fit companions for the angels above?

When my yearning heart fain would rend the veil
    that hides
  From my mortal vision the immortal gates of light,

I feel the touch of unseen hands reaching far, far
   down,
   And hear the rush of angel-pinions as they take
      their flight.

Perchance each strain of music, as it swells on yon-
   der shore
   And echoes far down the heavenly plains,
Is caught up on earth, and our fainting hearts
   Are cheered and soothed by the angelic strains.

Sometimes, when the din and battle of life
   Wax strong, and my dull, sluggish soul
Is enveloped in the darkness and blackness of night,
   And life's waters roll high, and its billows are cold,

Soft on my dulled ear steals a heavenly strain;
   Before my dimmed eye shines a vision of light;
Floats·the sweet music from the upper plains
   As it comes to me through the lonesome night.

Friends of my youth, I know that for me
   You wait just inside the portals of day;
And the love that was ours when you lingered here
   Will only be perfect in heaven away.

MY MOTHER'S GRAVE.

SOFTLY the summer-winds sigh o'er it
Throughout the long, still summer-hours;
The tall grass waves above with pleasant sound;
While purple daisies rear their modest flowers
Beside the gleaming, broken shaft that ever
Upward points where the rifting clouds
Float lightly, and melt away
Into a world of mist beyond the sunny hills.
A fair white rose, fit emblem of the soul
That only paused on the dull earth
To plume its wings, and take its flight
To eternity's fair and boundless shores,
Sheds an odorous fragrance round the sacred spot,
Where, in unbroken rest, she sleeps.
Long rifts of golden sunshine creep
Through the dense and shadowy foliage.
No sound breaks the solemn stillness save the robin's
　　song,

That rises sweet and clear upon the air;
Or the low, faint murmur of the rippling stream,
That ever ceaseless music makes, and onward flows
Across the forest-paths, down through fragrant vales,
With soft lulling sound, never pausing
Till its waters reach and mingle with the lake
That seems to slumber in the dim valley,
All shadowed by gigantic forest-trees.
And seasons roll their round.   Cold winter's blast
Sweeps by, and storm and tempest beat above the
    lowly mound.
Yet she seems not dead to me:
I hear her voice upon the summer-wind,
Her light step upon the rustling grass,
And see her smile upon the face of Nature;
And I know she walks the upper fields,
While that patient look she wore when here
Has radiant grown at the glory that surrounds her.

TO-MORROW.

WE are waiting, ever waiting,
For the morrow's dawn :
Pause we in the mystic gloaming
Ere the evening light has gone ;
And we say, " To-morrow's sunshine
Will be fairer than to-day's ; "
That to-morrow's bloom be brighter
When the hours have flown away.
And so slowly pass the moments !
Will the morrow never come ?
While through our grasp are slipping
The golden moments one by one.
Yet we fail to see their fleeing,
Their silent flitting on ;
And we say, " To-morrow will we gather
Richer, brighter gems ;
Cull from thoughtless pleasure
All the glamour that it lends ;

Never pausing in our watching
Till we reach the weary end."
Then we say the morrow's dawning
Never more can come :
Then the grave is wildly yawning ;
And, ere the day be done,
We shall be beyond all grieving,
In our Father's home.

THE AURORA BOREALIS.

SEE! — on yonder sky what pale, mysterious light
Is that, which, upward shooting, unveils the night,
Whose radial mellow hues the horizon spans,
From whence spring glittering crescent and deep
    auroral jets,
Wearing prismatic crown, whose swift-darting rays
Ever silent tend, where, on meridian heights,
Proud Venus twinkling shines with lesser glory,
Paling the tiny stars that form her train ;
While warlike Mars contends with all his strength
To shine undimmed, until at length

A soft glamour his lustrous brow o'erspreads?
He, too, succumbs to the strange power.
Now, defined 'gainst the horizon low, there gleams
A blood-red cross, surmounted by an anchor
Of pale amber hues, from whence leap up long belts
Of yellow flame, darting hither and thither,
Seeming in angry mood, that unquenched remains
Until to them shall be vouchsafed the power to soar
Onward into magnetic depths beyond their brilliant
 sisters,
Each wayward one vestment borrowing from
The inexhaustless source that upward streams
From globe terrestrial: while there rises
On the dazzled vision a mellowed blaze, comet-like
In fashion, far outward sweeping, quivering, per-
 turbed, and restless;
Semblance bearing to the meteor that its brilliance
Flashes o'er the trembling world for one brief moment,
And then retires to unknown realms
Beyond thought's penetration. So this mysterious
 form
Changes, amid the coruscating lights,
Into shapes undefined and luminous.
And mark how yon dim-hued shadows melt

Beneath the electric glow that is engendered
Within the sacred bosom of our common mother-
    earth,
From which outleaps an element mysterious,
Impalpable, and thin, gilding like
Ghostly visitant upward through the air,
In contact coming with a kindred current,
Soaring where the pale stars keep watch
In never-sleeping silence ; and the very rocks,
Whose adamantine hardness pierces the
Crustaceous mould, that is into fragments
Shivered by one electric blast,
Assume a shadowy grace in keeping with the scene.
Whence come ye, O pale, mysterious lights ?
Why choose these solemn, witching hours,
When all the world, in slumber buried,
Waketh not, your glitter to behold ?
On glacial regions, girt by eternal snows,
Gleam thy magnetic fires with gentler radiance ;
While the poor mariner, wedged 'mong massive
Minarets and towers of ice,
On thee gazes, thinking of that distant land
Which nevermore his weary feet may press ;
Sees, in that vision, eyes that have grown dim

With watching for the unreturning wanderer.
Science determines not the source from whence ye
    sprang:
Philosopher and hoary sage have bowed
The head in reverent wonder as o'er the world
Thou didst hang thy glittering coronet,
Leaving the impress of thy majesty
On all the land and mighty heaving sea,
While waiting for the hand of God
To draw aside the veil with which his wisdom
Shrouds the unopened labyrinths
That upward lead to gates of light.
So rest content, poor soul! for even now
Time in its swift flight comes bearing on its wing
A recompense for all thy longings;
For in the distance hovers a phantom
Dread and grim, who, unrelenting,
Waits for thee.   But shudder not,
Nor grow faint and cold: for on yon
Deathless shore is grouped
In countless numbers the angelic host;
And they shall welcome thy dazed soul
Into realms of eternal light and truth.

THOU ART NOT HERE.

THOU art not here! my soul is filled with sadness;
  Thou art not here!
Though all the earth is decked with gladness,
  And music steals upon mine ear,
And odors faint upon my sense,
  While sunshine flecks the mere
With shining belts that glint and glow,
While the wind sweeps by in murmurs low.

Thou art not here! Alone I wander
  Through fragrant summer-wood,
Heeding not its bloom ; while I silent ponder
  In melancholy mood
O'er the happy hours, the olden day,
  When our willing footsteps lightly strayed
  Down in the meadow, through the sunny glade,

Unmarking the moments flitting by,
Listening only to the murmuring sigh
Of the faint, sweet sounds of earth and sky.

And I turn my gaze to the fleecy rift
   That rests on the mountain's brow,
Or lightly float down to the low cliff
   Where the mists are rising now:
And a purple hue and shining light
Enshroud the valleys; while in misty white
Sleep the peaks beneath eternal snow,
Which no sunbeam can melt in its fervid glow.

And I call to the breeze, which answers me not;
   I call to the rushing river;
I whisper thy name to the forget-me-not
   That blossoms on the banks where the willows
      quiver;
And I say to the sunbeam, " Why shine to-day,
When one I love is so far away ? "

Unheeding me, the wandering breeze
Sighs in plaintive tones 'mong the forest-trees;

And the swift-rushing river pauses no more,
· But my questioning drowns in sullen roar,
While its silver waves lash the willow-lined shore.

And the sunbeam's glint and yellow glow
Wear a ghastly aspect; but soft and low
I hear in the distance a voice, whose tone
Chants this strain to me: " Thou art coming home."

WAITING.

HOPEFULLY waiting by the sea
For a ship that may never come to me;
Hopefully waiting in the dawn,
Catching a gleam of sun upon
My ship that sails like the morning star,
While the glimmering moon follows afar.

Hopefully I wait: the silver tide
Creeps at my feet; while far and wide,
All over the lichens, all over the wold,
The sunshine sleeps in mystic fold;
And I stoop to gather the pale sea-flower
That softly shines this silent hour.

Yet the sea rolls by; it rolls away.
O sea! hast thou seen my ship so gay?
It hath snowy sails, like a snow-white dove
That flitteth down from the heavens above.

The morn shone fair when my ship sailed away;
The breeze swept light o'er the placid bay.
My ship was bound for a summer-land;
And I hopefully wait on this ancient strand
To behold its white sails in the distance afar
Breasting the wave like the morning star.

Oh! angry and black now the clouds arise,
Infolding the sapphire of sunny skies;
Tempestuous winds begin to beat;
Swift the tide rolls at my feet;
Dread thunders break; the swelling sea
Dashes wildly up on the sandy lea.

There are breakers ahead! O ship! sail now,
While wild beat the billows around thy prow;
O ship! sail far, where the waters lie
Placid and deep as you drift by.

My ship hath gone down 'neath the ocean's surge ;
Loud moan the winds a solemn dirge :
Sadly I wait on the lonesome shore, —
Wait for the ship that can come no more.

Its wreck I gather from the cold, gray stones :
Dank weeds cling around ; a whirlpool foams ;
The boiling currents madly hiss now,
Dashing the spray around my brow.

Night closed around ; dread darkness fell ;
The winds shrieked aloud like a sudden knell ;
In inky blackness, as one vast plain,
The sea reposed ; and the desolate main
Repeated its echoes in sad refrain,
Till the hills took up the plaintive strain.

ADDRESSED TO DEITY.

Father, how grand thy works! The glorious sun
Floods all thy vast domains. • The earth, which
 smileth
Up to thee, clothed with all that's bright and good
 and fair, —
No blot rests on her face. The tiniest blade of grass,
The humblest flower that upward springs, bears token
Of thy wondrous power; while each into such grace
Is fashioned, that I pause, lost in thought's mysterious
Labyrinths, which comprehend not Nature's secret
 workings.
From her broad bosom a· thousand fragrant odors
 rise,
And incense sweet from all her lilies pale;
Her blushing roses, too, exhale perfumes
Faint and delicious, borne to me on balmy winds.
Seek yon mountain-heights, and behold what she has
 wrought!

Upon each uplifted brow a record stands of all the
  circling ages.
Some, tempest-rent and hoary, repose like warrior
Smitten by the battle into unwaking slumber;
And some are crowned with everlasting snows,
Upon which the sunlight rests, but softens never:
And yet a rosy glow oft infolds them, and purple
  mists;
While a fleecy cloud floats far above like some sweet
  angel
In its flight to heavenly shores.   And some she with
  unwearied hand
Scooped out into colossal basin, where, drop by
  drop,
The soft spring-rains fall, and melted snows; until at
  length
There stretched out a broad, blue lake, placid
Beneath the sky, at which there sippeth clouds,
And where the sun and moonbeams play; and so
  near the stars, that at night
They oft peep into its shadowy depths their glitter-
  ing forms
In proud array defined against the sky, and too de-
  fined

Upon its own unrippled bosom. On sandy plain
    remote, one

Awful peak uprises; and from its hollow depths
    come sounds

As if ten thousand cannons had belched forth terrific
    fires, and

Ten thousand groans issued from ten thousand hearts
    in agony;

And down its heated sides there rolls in one con-
    'tinuous mass ·

Molten lava, which the sickened earth ejects.

In cavern too, unlit by sun, her curious hand has
    wrought such

Curious veil wherewith to hide her mysteries! Some
    she hedges in

With marble walls, and paves the pathway to boiling
    caldron

With soft, calcareous earth, and illumines her vast
    domes

With pendants white and glittering; while uprise in
    gloomy

Labyrinths statues weird, all girt about with strange
    device, —

Monks in ashen cowl and flowing gown kneel at the
    altar,

And nuns in faded garments too, with rosary and
   beads
Counted never, yet looking as if death had overtaken
Them there, and chilled them into this great repose.
When we with sacrilegious foot would penetrate her
   inner sanctuary,
She unfolds her attendant ranks arrayed in rigid
   silence
To our gaze, so life-like, yet so pale, that one might
   think
That yestereve they walked and skipped about,
And shouted to each other, making the caverns dim
Resound with their wild melodies; while from each
   shining pendant
There falls a drop, which, perchance, is a tear shed
   by Mother Nature
For all her children who in secret weep.
Only the inconstant wind is a witness to her sighs,
   as it
Invades her realms.
O Father, how grand thy works! — the majestic sea,
   that
Sweeps in one broad belt from tropic shores crowned by
Summer suns and verdurous blooms, far out to frozen
   region

Girt by eternal snows, while its waves surge on past
    icy domes
And gleaming towers cold with the awful breath of
    a sunless winter,
But which sails by like a mighty moving palace in
    armament
Of glittering spears, yet unlike. For never a light
    shines
On moat or glacial battlement, each sentinel keeping
    watch
With hoary head, and eyelids fringed with frost-work,
Moveless and grim; nor sound of voice falls on the
    ear:
Only with awful crash the icy bodies meet like ships in
Battle, each concussion reverberating sounds through-
    out
Region lone, as if worlds had tumbled into chaotic
    mass together,
Deepening as it rolls away; while to its echoes the
    affrighted polar bear
Gives answer back, deeming it the distressful cry of
    mate
Upon a distant mountain. Ah! what is man, that he
    should cavil

In his feeble power, and strive to rear his palace on
    the plains,

Or gather from the bosom of thy vast earth her treas-
    ures,

Or bestride the mighty sea with mighty ships and

Lesser craft?   To-day his purple garments wrap him
    round :

Perchance they drip with blood wrung from widow's
    heart ·

And orphan's too. What matters it their royal tex-
    ture speaks of

Royal wealth, and all behold it? Ere the morrow's
    sun shall

Go down, his costly trapping laid aside, a shroud
    inwraps him,

And a sable pall : while among the heavenly hosts
    there rises not

A song of welcome; but a wail is heard in other
    realms, where dwell

The lost in everlasting darkness. Oh! why not seek
    to wrap the soul

Around with those sinless robes donated by a sinless
    Christ?

Why cry against the fallen, ".Unclean, unclean ! "

When the chamber that inshrines our souls is foul
· with malice,
And rank, evil thoughts, engendered by deceit and
. deadly envy, which
Spitteth forth its venom till all the air around is laden
With loathsome fungus taking root in other minds
like rank weeds
In some fair garden, blighting all the flowers? It
Chaseth out sweet Charity, until that angel takes her
flight forever :
Then we turn back aghast, veil our eyes, and rend
our hearts
With continuous cry for her return. Father, thus
thy world moves on.
But from Western wilds, from desert plains, and from
many a fair green field,
From cities vast, is heard humanity's feeble wail, as
its millions toil in gloom,
In sorrow toil, with grovelling souls that behold not
thee on shining heights,
But, untiring, seek amid the world's rush and din to
find the jewel thou
Holdest in thy grasp. Some souls look up as they
pass the boundary-line

That divides life and death, and, with cold, stiffening
    lips, seek
To relate the glorious vision. But to the faithful at
    last shall
Come joy, peace, and rest.
So be brave, poor heart! nor cast a backward glance,
But far upward raise thy vision to that
Land beyond the parting clouds that do but veil its
Brightness.

A LAMENT.

MORN breaks o'er the world how fair and sweet!
    While, from the east uprising,
The golden sun announces day,
    The tiny birds surprising
That were asleep 'mong the forest-trees
In nests all curtained by emerald leaves.

The hills wear a crown of sapphire mist;
    And the mountains grand and old
Above them hang, each brow intwined
    With purple clouds and gold:
From the ancient plains that stretch away
The shadows glide, so dull and gray.

The dew-drops glitter on the grassy blades
    In the heart of the opening flowers;
The breeze steals up from the mossy glades
    Through all the still, bright hours,
Wafting to me a fragrance sweet
From the budding blue-bells that ope to meet
The sun's bright glow, while it lightly unfolds
The poppies in their sleep.

But the earth that smiles, the flowers that bloom,
    And the softly murmuring breeze,
And the hills that sleep in sapphire mists,
    And birds that pipe in ancient trees,
Bring no joy to my heart, no joy to my life;
No sunshine's gold can gild its strife.
Cold, cold, its beams fall on my soul;
Cold, cold, the glancing rivers roll
Sounds in mine ear; the wild bird's song
A requiem is; while memories throng
Of olden days, and my buried dead,
Who silently come, and on my head
Place a spectral hand, then vanish away
Like shadows dim from the light of day.

No more shall I pause by the restless sea,
　And list to its wail and moan ;
No more shall I wander o'er the sandy lea
　That girt my childhood home,
Or gather from its rocks the lichens gray,
Or breathe the fragrance of its new-mown hay,
Or gather the rosebud from its shining tree,
　Or pluck the lily's waxen bells,
Or chase the butterfly over the lea
　And down through the woody dells,
Or gather the sea-weed when the tide rolls out,
Or the ocean shells from the sands about.

Here the tempest may beat, or the sun may shine,
　The flowers may wither, or the flowers may bloom,
The birds may pipe 'mong the ancient trees,
　And the mountains uprise in light or gloom.
Oh ! my love lies dead by the sounding sea ;
While the waves creep up o'er the sandy lea,
And wildly beat, and foam at his feet,
Shrouding his grave like a winding-sheet.

　Once I paused by the ancient sea :
　　The red moon hung on high ;

A blazing star shone red on me
　From out the midnight sky;
The sluggish tide it crept like blood
　Beating in wild monotones,
Whelming beneath its sickening flood
　The lichens that clung to the gray stones.
How it curled at my feet,
And restlessly beat!
Now whirling back in mad retreat,
　Then leaping and creeping,
　Then wailing and weeping
　Unto the moon, red vigils keeping
Unto the stars in the amber sky,
　Unto the sea in weird tones repeating
The echoes that woke on the hills anigh.

Wearied I sank upon the fallow lea,
And thus addressed the lamenting sea: —
" O sea! were yon moon a globe of blood
　Hung up in yonder sky,
And I could cast it in thy flood,
　And all the stars anigh,
O restless sea! O moaning sea!
What wouldst thou then restore to me?"

But unanswering whirled its mocking tide
All over the sea-walls far and wide.
Then a song I sang to the sounding sea,
Weary reclining on the fallow lea,
While the moon shone red on the gory stones,
And the waves beat up in wild monotones,
And long arms flung like blood-red bands
Around and across the yellow sands.

I sang, " O sea! under thy fretful tides
   One lieth asleep,
With the gold o' noon in her silken hair;
   And unto her frozen feet
The garnered wealth of many years
   Is piled in glittering heap;   .
And a coral palace stretcheth wide,
   And coral caverns deep.

" O cruel sea, O lamenting sea,
Winding past the fallow lea !
Thy crested billows' swell
Soundeth like a funeral-knell;
And thy pink and tiny shells

Seem like drops of blood .
Under the blood-red moon,
   Hurled by thy boiling flood
Up from her soundless tomb."

But the sea, that answered me not,
   Whirled lamenting by ;
While the stars grew pale and soft
   Up in the amber sky ;
And the moon's red light
   Resolved to paly gold
Its electric flood ; the waning night
   Drew round in glittering fold ;
While the fretful tide o'er the yellow sands,
Gleaming, shot like silver bands.

And voices chanted on the purple hills ;
   The voice of bird and bee
Mingled with the wind's low trills
   Unto the remorseless sea ;
Across the sky a gold banner hung,
   Parted by crimson bands ; .
And sheets of flame far upward flung,
   Upheld by unseen hands.

While methought from the glory there sprung,
  Far down to the ocean sands,
A presence so sweet, that the tide at my feet
  Drew back in pale affright:
All the sounding sea, all the fallow lea,
  Quick caught its holy light.

And the ocean that rolled o'er curls o' gold,
  O'er a form o' grace asleep,
And the waves that coil in icy fold
  Unto her frozen feet,
Enchain not her soul, now on other shore,
  Walking the pearly street,
With a dazzled vision that discerns evermore
  The glory at her feet.

And up I rose from the fallow lea,
Singing no more to the petulant sea
That defiantly moanèd back to me,
But gazed afar, where the rising sun
Proclaimed to me a day begun,
And all the sea it shone upon;
While green rolled its waves over the stones,
Beating about in low monotones.

TO LITTLE LIDA.

O LITTLE hands forever folded!
　O little feet at rest!
O soft blue eyes that ope not!
　O brow I oft have pressed!

O glossy, silken tresses
　Lying beneath the mould,
Under the ferns and grasses,
　Under the daisy's gold!

How much of sin and sorrow,
　How much of pain or bliss,
How many a sad to-morrow,
　Thy baby heart has missed!

O voice whose plaintive music
　Is hushed forevermore!
O parted lips, and pallid!
　My heart is grievèd sore

That all the blight and mildew
   Of death hath folded round;
That all thy grace and comeliness
   Is mouldering in the ground.

But up among the angels
   Thy spirit wanders free
'Mid the golden streets, the jasper,
   And by the silver sea.

Thy snowy raiment floateth
   Like a blaze of glory down;
On thine angel brow there resteth
   A radiant golden crown.

O hearts on earth that mourneth !
   Look up to worlds of light
Where angel Lida dwelleth,
   Hid from your yearning sight.

A DREAM.

DREAD darkness fell upon my senses, and my
Inward vision wandered far out to unknown realms.
Before me stretched a plain of inky blackness,
Where no flower blossomed, no dews fell;
But swept by one continuous wind, whose
Clammy breath ever bore the slimy essence
That may come forth from charnel-house,
Or yawning grave where human bones
Lie rotting.   Through all the plains there rolled
A sluggish stream, whose waves slow hissed,
And bubbled up o'er rocks that lay like
Mountains in their midst; and lakes like
Cesspools lay, deep and black, which the
Clammy winds disturbed not;
Whose banks shot up devoid of living thing,
Of shrub or tree devoid, and far out
Into blank space retiring.   Trembling I stood;
For dreadful thunders rolled, shaking the

Vast plain on its foundations. Great chasms
Opened wide their jaws; flames leaped up,
As if the fires of hell had burst their
Confines; and the very smoke into forms
Resolved, and shapes strange and hideous,
That mocked me with their fiery eye,
And strove with fiery feet to climb
The leaping flames. Now the river rose
To beat it down, and flung its sluggish
Tides amid the raging heats that higher,
Higher rose, and shrieked and raved,
Drowning the reverberating thunder's voice.
A lake, that heretofore had stood still,
Arose, and its slimy contents poured
O'er all the raging flames, until the fiery,
Horrid shapes shot out in frenzied madness;
And the fire-tongued monsters wild beat it
Down. Each in awful merriment held up
A flaming hand, as from the emptied
Lake there issued groans and shrieks of
Horrid laughter. A bell began to toll:
A thousand brazen bells ne'er clanged so
Loud, so slow, so deep. One tone I heard:
It might have been oceans raging in

Their maddest fury, or worlds crushed out,
Or meteors whirling by.   Another tone: it
Might have been the groan of ten ·'
Thousand damnèd souls mingled into
One.   But deeper still upon mine ear
Did fall another, mournful at first, then
Breaking into a wail, as if God's judgment-
Day had come ; and from out the
Sea the risen dead called unto the mountains
And unto the unrelenting rocks to hide
Them from his wrath.   Then louder pealed
Its brazen tongue o'er all the plain ; the fiery
Monsters hid ; the leaping flames retired
Aghast ; the shrinking river its hiss
And bubble ceased ; but blew the
Slimy winds continuously with the breath
Of charnel-house and open grave.
Heated was all the plain ; and, lo !
In its midst a mountain towering rose,
Girdled around with awful grandeur.
No living thing was seen ; no verdurous robes
Encrowned its sides ; no tree spread its
Branches o'er the stones ; no babbling
Stream flowed downward to the plains :

But blistered lava-rocks blistered the
Smoking earth, which, in return, seemed
The slimy air to blister; till in one
Great convulsion all the chasms closed,
And the sluggish river, scorched into
Dryness, sank amid the sands.   Now night
Came on; and such a night!   Uprose the
Moon like one red globe of blood.
The stars glittered like sharp rays of
Steel, and seemed to dart in madness
O'er the sky.   High hung a cloud above
The massive mount; until, in sudden anger, from
Its cracked jaws there burst huge jets of flame,
That shot forth with dreadful hiss, boiling
And sputtering like a mighty caldron
Fed by the very fires of hell, thundering
Forth with one continuous sound, drowning
The clamorous-pealing bell; and the thick,
Sulphurous smoke rolled, and, beaten
By the slimy winds, hid in
Its awful folds the blood-red moon:
But still the stars, emitting their steely
Fires, glimmered through the darkness.
Nought else was seen save the lurid

Fires, which might be kindled
Down where damnèd spirits hold
Their revels; and, half hid by coils
Of smoke, looked hellish.
But while the darkened moon struggled feebly 'mid
The fiery flood; while volcanoes
Burst, drowning the thunder's voice,
Shaking the plains, and seemed
To throttle all the staring stars, —
I trembling stood, striving to
Blind my vision to the gaping lava
Sea, and shutting from my senses
All this warring strife.   And, lo! upon
Mine ear there stole a whisper; so
Faint at first, that I comprehended not
Its import.   Then it grew sweet and
Loud, until it swelled into one grand
Anthem, so like the songs chanted by the angels
On the blessed hills, and which reached
Far down, and broke
Clear and sweet above the plains
Where watched the shepherds.   My
Inthralled senses stood still.   The
Moon stood still; all her fierce

Red beams resolved into a soft,
Silver radiance. Sudden, as if a
Magic wand had swept the plains,
Trees uprose, and budding flowers ;
While methought I caught the faintest
Echoes of a rippling stream, and the
Soft dash of limpid waves against
A moss-lined shore. I heard the wind
Swell plaintive on the hills, and
Felt its balmy breath cooling my
Heated brow ; while, lo ! upon
My entranced vision burst a
Reflex of such glory, — only the reflex, —
That all my soul grew dumb.
Methought 'twas morn. The risen
Sun stood still, draped with banners
Wrought with gold, and canopied
With purple mists which
Half hid its wondrous brightness ;
When suddenly there burst a blaze
Of glory from its midst. The
Parting clouds fled on. The amazed
Earth quivered with delight. The King
Of kings sat on his throne ; and

By his side was *One* who looked
On me with such tender grace,
That my whole soul arose, clad,
Methought, in those spotless robes
Washed white in his own precious blood.

SOLILOQUY.

WHO says life "is a fevered dream;"
The world a dull stage,
Whereon poor actors take a part,
Fretting their souls in feeble rage
Till Death with stony grasp
Fastens them unto eternal slumber,
Wherein no dream uncloses the frozen lids,
No trembling breath awakes the sleeper,
No voice of love calling from afar
Can break upon the ear?
Alas! who knows? The spark
That fed the fires of immortality
Which so feebly glimmered up amid

The shadows — its exit from this
Cold lump of clay none witnessed:
Its destination — where, oh! where?
In what mysterious shape it took its flight?
How fled?   Did other spirits bear it
Up to worlds of light? or did it sink
In everlasting darkness?
Here lies the form of one I loved,   .
So changed, cold, and mysterious!
At all my eager questionings
The frozen lips unclose not;
The eye, wont to smile back on me,
Answers now with fixed, unmeaning stare;
The fires lit beneath it have gone
Out: but where, oh! where,
The hand that idled not amid the day?
It's folded o'er the frozen heart.   Only
The silken tresses lie unchanged.
The rose, whose fragrant breath
Might wake the heaviest slumberer,
Lies light upon the brow,
Whose marble fixedness might
Put to shame the fairest image e'er
Called into being by the hand of man.

Cold, cold, unmeaning silence,
Whose mysteries I cannot penetrate,
And so forbear.   Leaving ye,
I go back to life, which is not life
Without thee.
Yet one blessed thought strikes me, —
That, when this frozen mantle falls on
Me, thou canst not weep
As I am weeping.

CAST UP BY THE WAVES.

DEAD!   Upon her upturned face
The pale moonlight lingered ;
Upon her unbound hair, whose
Long, dark waves, matted with dank
Weeds and ocean-shreds, clung round
The marble neck and brow as
It tangled lay
Upon the rocks ; while ever and anon
The cruel waves crept up, and stirred
Its silken folds, as oft upon a summer
Day it stirs a rose-leaf.

Swift the marshalling clouds swept
O'er the sky ; swift the ocean-tides
Rolled on ; loud and deep, in
Clamorous tones, the breakers thundered
O'er the rocks, and, like a deep bassoon,
Called out and shrieked and raved,
Till on the angry ocean's lips stood
Great flecks of foam, which lightly
Danced far out upon the shore until
They bore the look of tiny seas afloat,
Whose framework might be blood.
Dead, and alone !   The winds
Might beat ; the angry sea cast
Up its flecking form ; the moon
Peer down upon the ghastly scenes,
And shed its melancholy flood
Upon the marble pallor of the
Brow, and lips just parted with
A smile ;
Voices from over the sea might
Call, and that great sea repeat the
Call in vain : for in such dreamless
Slumber hath it wrapped her round,
Though it shrieked out in remorseful

Cries until it rent the very skies,
Yet would no answer
Come from the pallid lips;
No motion as if the pale feet might
Seek to wander by the shore.
Cast up by the waves,
And lying on the cold
Gray rocks, with rounded limbs
In attitude of grace composed; one
Dimpled arm across her breast; and
Yet her tiny feet are folded
With that awful fixedness which
To death alone belongs.
O cruel sea! O cruel tide! ye had
No mercy on the fragile child, but beat
And beat, and chilled the life-blood
In her tender veins;
But in the dreadful night, when,
Above the blackness, angels watched
For her pure soul's exit, methinks
They bore it in calmness up to God.

LINES ON THE BIRTHDAY OF A FRIEND.

SOFTLY the sun of this fair morning
    Comes up from the ancient hills;
And its white beams lend a gentle grace
    To barren plain and frozen rills.

In the distance the mountains tower,
    Sublime, mysterious, and old;
While light, fleecy clouds are floating above,
    Mingled with purple and gold;

And the cool west-wind is murmuring
    An anthem low and sweet,
All idly roving, and softly lingering
    Where plain and mountain meet.

My friend, I pause, on this fair morning
    That ushers in thy natal day,
To breathe a prayer of glad thanksgiving
    To my Father in heaven away, —

That he in his goodness hath lent thee
　　To grace this fair, sweet earth :
My heart in its joy reverently wonders
　　If angels rejoiced at its birth.

Noble soul ! with the redeemed may you stand,
　　Crowned with everlasting life,
On that day when Death claims you for his own,
　　And ends all mortal strife !

And if, in the dim, uncertain future,
　　Your faltering feet may tread
Life's thorny way in bitterness, remember our Sa-
　　　　viour
　　Had not where to lay his head.

And lift your eyes beyond the hills,
　　Where the golden gates of morning
For your entrance will be opened wide   ·
　　Into life's eternal dawning.   .

D A Y.

CREEPING o'er the mountain
  With all her rosy train;
Flushing field and fountain;
  Flooding all the main
With purple lights, the golden;
  Wreathing a glittering chain
Around the mountain olden,
  Around the ancient plain;

Brightening all the river;
  Changing the old gray stones
Into molten silver,
  Gleaming like liquid domes, —
Round eternal snows a mantle
  Of luminous, glowing red
She inwrappeth, soft and gentle
  As roses round the dead.

The clouds up in the heavens
　　Might be the gates that fold,
And shut from our yearning vision
　　The streets of pearly gold;
So strange is all their beauty,
　　So lustrous and so bright:
Oh! is that wondrous city
　　Hidden from mortal sight?

Oh! is that sea that shineth,
　　Oh! is that waveless sea
That midst the city lieth
　　In golden, placid splendor, —
Is it fairer than yon sky,
　　Hung o'er with radiance tender,
With glory from on high?

O unseen spirits that wander
　　Earthward with message of love!
Oh! speak of the land up yonder, —
　　The land that shines above;
The sun that breaketh in glory
　　Over the dull gray world;
The clouds, marshalling all slowly,
　　Like rainbow banner unfurled;

And tell me if heaven be fairer
　　Than gold and amber skies :
The light that falls — oh ! is it rarer
　　Than morning in this guise ?

HOW MANY SILENT VOICES !

How many silent voices
　　Hath the silent night ! —
In the wind that tosses
　　The leaves all alight ;

In the voice of stars ablaze
　　Up in the measureless sky ;
In the voice of waning moon
　　Majestic sailing by ;

And the dwellers in the sea ;
　　The sea-flower pale below ;
The wave of voiceless tree ;
　　The rose like drift of snow.

List! I hear them all,
  As through the solemn night
Soft and sweet they call,
  Like viewless things of light.

Oh! the angels are abroad,
  And in the dimness sweep
A misty radiance round my head,
  A glory at my feet.

IN EXILE.

DAY wanes; and stealthy night inwraps
Its sombre shadows round the busy human tide
Which all day have surged through the crowded ways,
Remorselessly beating 'gainst the feeble waifs
Cast wrecked and worn upon the shores of Time,
Their semblance of humanity crushed out,
As obstacles that rise in the way of its advancement, —
Perilled and bartered souls, who can date
Their downfall to this fair-seeming day,
Lured by some treacherous, shining wave

Which bore upon its bosom the richest garniture of
 years,
And that priceless jewel, Honor,
Which, once relinquished, no tidal wave
In the dim, receding years upheaves.
But, alas ! beneath its surge and roll
Long belts of cold gray rock
And treacherous quicksands lay,
'Mong which a whirlpool circled,
Eddying round, opening its jaws rapacious,
Seeking to ingulf 'neath the sounding waves
A soul, leaving the casket tenantless.
And now the shadows deepen,
Until the stately look dim ;
While just beyond rise the towering summits
Of the Rocky range, crowned with eternal snows,
That whitely gleam, and mingle
With the parting clouds, until my vision fails to scan
Where mountains end, and clouds begin ;
While above, like a tiny jewel set in Night's
Regal diadem, one glimmering star peeps forth,
Hanging low upon the mountain's brow
In mystery and sublimity.
My soul delights in all this beauty, and yet

Is chilled with the plaintive, melancholy sound
Of the wind that comes from the distant
Heights, bearing on its wings odors from
Unnumbered blossoms and vinous shrubs,
Faint and delicious, wrapping the senses round
Like subtle perfume borne from Eastern land.
Each bird has sought its leafy couch, —
Some among the whispering pines; while the
Chaffinch and oriole are
Lulled into repose in the swaying,
Ancient poplars.   I hear the river
Rush all along the gleaming sands,
And see its waters wandering far down
The plain, till, lost in the interminable stretch,
It rolls away, commingling with its sister-streams.
A faint glow o'erspreads the eastern hills,
Semblance bearing to the rosy hues of morn;
While I see the crescent Moon rise up in all
Her glory, and walk the heavens a queen.   ·
My spell-bound vision no longer ranges,
But dwells with lingering gaze
Upon the radial lights that shoot
Across the heavens, scattering the clouds,
And piercing through mists that

Settled o'er the valley; glancing on
The lake's unrippled surface;
Flecking with long, shining bars its margin,
All adorned with creeping vines,
And roses wild just bursting into bloom.
Ah! sweet Night, thou trailest thy shadowy
Vestments over land and restless sea;
Drawing thy mighty veil athwart the vision;
Hiding Day's brighter glories, yet revealing
Dimly its beauties, mellowed and
Toned down, until each object bearing
Animate life seems lulled into repose,
And a sadness deep steals o'er me
As the solemn hours flit by;
And olden memories come as shadows in the sky
Of the royal land that gave me birth, its
   Shaded vales and streams,
Where the blossoming hillside caught
   Its rosy, purplish gleams
From the sun's red glow, that kissed
   The opening flowers,
And beams on them with steadfast ray
   Throughout the summer-hours.
And I wander an exile evermore. No land

Can seem so fair ;
No other sunshine gleam on me with
    Such a radiance rare ;
No other friend give greeting so tender
    And so kind ;
No other token seem so sweet
    As this token that I find
Within memory's deep, still chambers,
    Where, sleeping never more,
Its tenants wait for signal
    From yonder deathless shore.

THE MUNE SHINES BRIGHT. .

Oh! saft and sweet the new mune shines
    Abune the cauld, gray plains ;
Oh! saft and sweet the wind's low chimes
    Brak' into sad refrains.

The mountains rise wi' crest o' snow
    To meet the bendin' skies ;
Far in the west a bricht star glows,
    And blinks wi' shinin' eyes

Upo' the warld, the dreary warld,
    That brak' my heart long sin';
While yon gret cloud unco furled
    Round the mune a silver rim.

Wi' shinin' eyes a' the lesser stars
    Gang down the milky-way,
And smilin' back on bluidy Mars
    Lik' tiny warlds at play.

O luvly mune! O luvly nicht!
    O blinkin', blinkin' star,
Ashinin' up in the heavens sae bricht
    Abune the hills afar!

Will ye nae gie my sorry heart
    A robe as pure as the lilies' snow,
Sae, when angels ca' me in the dark,
    Their voices I sure shall know?

And in sinless garments I lay me down,
    While the sweet young mune may shine,
And cast on my grave a wilderin' crown,
    And my lowly bed inshrine

Wi' a halo o' glory sae pure and bright,
　　That footsteps passin' nigh
Sha' tread sae saftly, sha' tread sae licht,
　　Nor unco weep nor sigh ;

But, as they gither a rose wi' luvin' hand
　　From out its sister fold,
They'll think o' me 'mid the shinin' band
　　That wa'k the streets o' gold.

PARTED.

SOUNDS of laughter, sounds of music,
　　Mingled with the voices' hum ;
Gleam of jewel, flash of gaslight,
　　As the thronging memories come.
Oh ! the halls are wide in my palace fair ;
But heavy my heart with dole and care.

Within yon room are dancing feet
Keeping time with music sweet ;

And the voices flow and hum
As the thronging memories come.
Oh! my palace-halls are wide and fair;
But heavy my heart with dole and care.

Once I paused 'neath the maples' glow,
In the olden time, in the long-ago:
Crimson and gold the leaves
Lay at my feet; the yellow sheaves
The reapers bound in the fields away;
The purple mists o'er the valley lay;
And the forest-aisles, with garlands gay,
Were all aflame this autumn-day.

I said, "Farewell!" the skies grew dim;
  "Farewell!" echoed the fields;
The daisies paled round their purple rim
    As the sound died away in mournful peals;
The wind sobbed low; the sob of the pine
In harmony blent like the mystic chime.

There was a clasp of hands that nevermore
Shall clasp in meeting on earth's dim shore;
Footsteps paused 'neath the maples' glow
In that olden time, that long-ago,

When the skies were bright, and then grew dim,
And the pines sobbed aloud, while the winds crept
    in ;
Around the circling sun a cloud
Inwrapped its white mantle like a shroud.

Over the seas one sailed away,
    Robbing the day of its gold, —
Sailed away where tropic bay
    Placid waves in silver fold.
Oh ! my palace-halls are wide and fair ;
But heavy my spirit with dole and care.

I stand beneath the star-gemmed sky,
While the round white moon sails slowly by ;
And I hear the music's swell ;
    And the dancing feet
    To its melody do beat ;
And like a solemn knell
The sound of that farewell,
And one who sailed away
O'er silver sea to tropic bay,
The maples' glow, the yellow sheaves,
The crimson and gold of autumn-leaves.

I see the sheen of my bridal robes;
   And the orange-flowers infold
The misty veil that floateth down
   Like web of transparent gold;
The form of stately grace I see;
The look of love that's bent on me;
Words I hear, tender and sweet,
Crushing the lilies 'neath my feet,
Scattered by one who loved me well
Ere I spoke that last farewell.
Oh! my palace-halls are wide and fair;
But heavy my heart with dole and care.

My hair is black as the raven's wing;
   But blacker the shadows in my soul,
As it peers through the darkness, shutting in
   Its sorrow and its dole:
While high above the melody there swell
The echoes of that sad farewell;
   And the dancing feet,
     And the laughter gay,
   And the music sweet,
     In the halls away,
   Hath a mocking tone,
   Like a moan or groan;

And a spectre haunteth me
   Of one who sailed away
   O'er silver sea to tropic bay.
Oh! my palace-halls are grand and fair;
But heavy my soul with dole and care.

O silver sea! O tropic bay!
   Waft to the flower-girt shore
One memory of that autumn-day
   That cometh back no more.
Is the stately head bent low,
   Or lifted in love and light,
Soft o'er the heart will steal, I know,
   Memories fair and bright
Of a bride at the altar; the autumn-leaves,
And the reapers binding the yellow sheaves,
And the trees aflame in the forest-aisle;
Of the heart that loved without a guile;
Of the farewell spoken 'neath the glow
Of the bending maples long ago.

LIFE AND DEATH.

MORN stood just within Night's portals,
　And gently forth did peep,
As if afraid of rousing Earth's mortals
　Up from their quiet sleep:
But her pale beams lit all the valley
　And the lone mountain's steep;
And the wind began to sigh mournfully,
　Rippling the lakelets deep,
Music making through the rocky chasm;
　Waking the violets meek,
Shaking the dew-drop from their velvet petals;
Sweeping odors from the silver-maples;
　Stooping to kiss the opening rose;
　Wandering where the buttercup blows.
And luminous was all the sky
　With a pale amber light,
And wore her radiant, fleecy robes
　With a grace so bright!

The glorious sun tipped tree and flower
   And emerald vales;
The lark's song rose high, and blended with
   The melodious nightingale's.
This morning ushers in
   Death and Life,
Each warring with the other
   In melancholy strife.
Side by side, hand in hand,
Pause they not on Earth's dim strand,
Each possessed with mystic wand, —
One tipped with life, the other manned
With that ghastly thing called Death;
And from its nostrils one icy breath
   Forever freezes and forever chills
   The eye that sparkles, the heart that thrills:
But the soul looks up o'er the battle's din
To the glory beyond that it's sure to win.

MIDNIGHT.

THE hush of midnight rests in solemn gloom
  O'er all the world asleep;
While, slowly sailing on, the majestic moon
  Out from the ragged clouds doth peep,
Leaving long belts of mellow light,
  Silvering the solemn plain,
Piercing through the shades of night,
  And moving in her train
Of stars that glitter and softly glow
With lesser light on the earth below.
Dimly in the distance the mountains I trace;
  While to their hoary crests
The moonlight lends a glamour and grace
  As it lightly on them rests.
There is a charm in this midnight-hour
  That speaks to all my soul;
A peaceful calm, a sacred power,
  Through all its portals roll;

And I see in the moon, I see in the clouds,
   I see in each glimmering star,
And plains that sleep in shadow-like shrouds
   And stretch in the distance afar,
The great Architect's power, the mighty hand,
The voice that speaks in tones so grand,
Yet so small and still, that while I list,
And my spirit keeps its lonely tryst,
The hours have fled, the midnight's gone,
And gray light heralds the coming morn.

THE SUICIDE.

DESPAIRING and homeless, she fled
   Out in the cheerless night:
No pitying angel her footsteps stayed
   In their mad, reckless flight.

Yet the stars shone on as they ever shine;
   And shone the crescent moon;
Its silver light fell on each nook and dell
   Fragrant with summer bloom.

All through night's silence came the sound
   Of the sullen, restless sea,
As it ever rolled on with quiver and moan
   Like a lost soul in agony.

'Neath its blue waves she sought repose :
   How softly they closed around,
And quickly enshrouded her fair, frail form,
   With so many graces crowned !

The tide rolled in, the tide rolled out ;
   On the yellow sands she lay ;
Dank seaweed twined in her golden hair ;
And in her blue eyes death's stony glare :
But a smile dwelt on lip and face so fair,
As angels had left their impress there,
   And flown with her soul away.

A POEM ON THE SEA.

ONCE I paused in the evening tide
    On the majestic ocean's shore:
The clouds across the heavens did ride;
    And the moon began to pour
A luminous flood on the restless waves,
    As they beat with sullen roar
O'er the yellow sands, the shifting sands,
    And beat and beat evermore.

Afar and away rose the stately hills,
    Crowned with soft gray light;
While shining rifts of moonshine crept,
    Like clouds of silvery white,
Across the marsh and across the brake,
    That seemed asleep this solemn night.

And my vision soared where a million stars
  Twinkled, and glimmering shone
With radiance soft, while following afar
  In the wake of the glittering moon;
And the cold winds swept the salt seaweed
  That dank and lifeless lay
Where the treacherous tide that morn had lured
  It up from the sunken bay.

And the solemn beauty that grandly robed
  The majestic earth and sky
Surged through my brain and wandering soul
  Like echoing strains that never die;
That cliff repeat, and answering cave,
  Until their last and faintest sigh
Seems among the clouds and among the stars
  And the zephyrs sweet that wander by.

8

SOLD.

THESE jewels flash and gleam to-night,
 Mocking my soul's agony,
Wreathing, twining, clasping so tight,
 While the hours laggingly
Pass on Time's dull and tedious wings,
That back on my heart silently flings
Memories that Lethe's mystical wave,
Though all its drowsy waters should lave
 This secret sanctuary,
Could never lull into unbroken sleep
The Past's dim cadence that o'er me sweeps ;
And I had garnered and kept with jealous care,
 In a rich repository,
A clustered gem, so sweet and fair,
With glamour laden, and so rare,
That my dazed soul took·only in
The paler shine of its golden rim.

One day I lost it in the whirl and rush,
     In the battle's din:
In vain I seek, my heart to hush,
     My jewel back to win.
To-night I sit in my halls of mirth,
Feeling within a melancholy dearth;
Seeking ever for that inner light
Which gave to my soul a new birthright:
So these jewels, that flash and gleam
     On my brow mockingly,
Ever point, through the years that chime
     In the halls of memory,
To that far past, wherein my soul,
Unsoiled, sought the shining goal
That lured me on with illusive show,
And beckoned me with its illusive glow.
Corroding care sits at the springs
     Of my life sullenly,
Heeding not what bitterness it brings,
     Nor what melancholy:
A phantom it sits at every feast,
Seemingly counting each bidden guest.
When merriment noisily creepeth in,
It ever looks on with ghastly grin;

Its ghoul-like eyes emitting a light
Which falls on my heart with terrible blight.
Its reflection I see in the emerald's gleam
  That mingles shiningly
With the diamond's glimmering sheen,
  And gold wrought cunningly,
Interlaced and woven with curious skill.
This bracelet I clasp with undefined thrill,
As if fearing the touch of a cold, dead hand
'Twixt that of mine and this fettering band.
The world, envying my glitter and gold,
  Looks on smilingly,
Heeding not the heart's wealth sold,
  Like a miser, grudgingly;
While I see in its hollow praise,
'Neath all its false and delusive ways,
This spectre pale who mocketh all,
Shrouding my heart like a funeral-pall.

THE OLD CHURCH.

It was a day in spring-time. Earth smiled,
And donned her flowing robes with such royal grace
As might befit a queen. On this day, within the por-
　　tals
Of a time-worn church, I idly wandered;
While through its dim aisles phantoms of the fair,
　　sweet past
Yet lingered like the echoes of a pleasant melody.
Through its windows, ivy-wreathed and stained,
A sunbeam glanced, and on the sacred altar rested,
Where nevermore should sound
The voice of praise or prayer, lending
A gentle radiance to its decay, and dispelling
The shadowy twilight that lingered there.
Through the ancient portals and open door
The fresh winds softly came, all laden
With the wild flowers' fragrance. Outside, the mourn-
　　ful pine —

That, even on the brightest summer's day,

Sighs as if with some secret pain —

Waved its branches, and still moaned on.

I passed within the ancient chancel, and pictured

How, in days gone by, had gathered there

The young, the gay, the happy,

The aged, and sorrow-stricken too ;

And how the infant at the baptismal font

Had received the holy blessing.

All, all, had passed away, —

Some in life's fair young morning ;

And some had aged grown

Ere they were called to heaven ;

Some toiled in other lands :

But all, at last, should don death's cerements.

And I fancied the broken organ-keys,

Touched by unseen hands, sent forth harmonious
    strains,

With which were mingled voices from an angel-band.

It was a dream ; but around me evermore

Memories of that day will softly linger,

Till time, never pausing in its flight,

Will bring about the longed-for hour

When I shall sing beyond the gates of paradise.

THE APACHE.

WHERE Gila's mount of black basalt
    Rears to the skies its hoary crest,
Flinging weird lights on the lower hills
    That stretch away in silent rest,
Down to the valley where Gila's stream
Flows swiftly on with ripple and gleam,
.In untrammelled freedom the dread Apache
    Mounts his flying steed, and hies away
O'er desert plains and barren wastes,
    Like a wingèd demon all astray ;
In ambush halts, with gloating soul,
Till the shades of night shall o'er him roll ;
Then, sneaking, he glides amid the rocks.
In his downcast eye mad murder gleams ;
His tongue the cunning serpent's tongue ;
His gravity deep, a mocking screen
That hides from his unwary foe
How treachery strikes its fatal blow.
.In hollow dens and hidden caves
    By day he lurks with death intent,

Smiling grimly when his victim falls

    From the arrow's poison so stealthily sent ;

While he with gory and glittering blade

Severs from the head of the murdered maid

Her silken locks that look like gold,

Clasping her round in shining fold.

Now bloody warrior and hag-like squaw,

    With impish babe and elfish child,

With knotty fagot and brush and brake,

    All gather in the forest wild ;

While their howls rise shrill and high

On the affrighted breeze that wanders by.

And the victim they bind to the burning stake,

    With pitiless torture prolonging his life ;

Cutting and piercing his quivering flesh ;

    Striving still with mortal strife,

Each seeking some new, awful mode

To dabble in his curdled blood ;

Screeching if they rend a groan

    From his cold and clammy lips,

While, oozing from unnumbered wounds,

    The crimson tide all slowly drips ;

While they whirl around with terrible din,

Dancing the death-dance with hellish vim,

Till their dread orgies o'er all that remains
  Is a dimly-smouldering heap
Of embers dead ; while, above, the stars
  Glimmeringly seem to keep
A mournful watch, and the white moonbeams
Peer through the shades in fitful gleams,
While they coilèd sleep in a clump of pines,
  Like the filthy cur who rends the night
'With snarling bark and whine prolonged,
  While he howls out his affright
If a leaflet is stirred by the sighing breeze
As it skips about 'mong the forest-trees.
His soul delights in wampum-belt
  All thickly studded with shining beads ;
While pendent hangs the ghastly scalp, —
  Trophies of his murderous deeds ;
While in secret he scans the mingled locks
With the greedy eye of a hungry fox.
Each tribe owns a doctor, or medicine-man,
  That like a mystic divinity dwells
Alone in a tepe, where he converse holds ·
  With bogies that haunt the caves and fells ;
While his hideous face more hideous seems,
All streaked with red and horrible greens.

When, swooping down with invisible wing,
  Death woes him into eternal sleep,
And his soul is gone to the " hunting-grounds,"
  Where it, mayhap, will meet
Its own wild steed, and bestride him there,
Unjaded, unfettered, fleet, and fair;
While the body's suspended upon a limb,
  And magpie and raven peck
At his staring eyes, and seem to gloat
  O'er the morsels they steal from his fleshless
    neck;
His only shroud the soft emerald leaves
That cluster around on the forest-trees.
This is the life of the noble " red man "
  Who roams the Western plains;
This the prowess of which poets have sung
  In their loftiest, sweetest strains;
While with reeking hand and murderous heart
Retires to his mountain-fastness all apart,
And, unmolested, gloats o'er his stolen hoard
With fury unabated, and memory all stored
With invented wrongs and treacherous hate
Which no blood of " pale-face " can ever sate.

MELODY.

A MELODY I heard : 'twas like the songs
  That swell on the heavenly plains.
And upward I gazed till the angel-throng
  That chanted these sweet refrains
Seemed to break on my vision ; the gates of gold
All backward swung in shining fold ;
And, crowned with pearl, their pillars white
Uprose by a sea of dazzling light.

There was no day, there was no change ;
  But the floods of glory sweeping down
In endless brightness grew so strange,
  That all the earth seemed crowned
With holy radiance ; and the sun
Abashèd hid ere his course was run,
Till the stars came out, till the sweet young moon
Hung high above the fields of June.

Still then on the mountains there lingered a light;
On the emerald plains e'en the shadows grew bright;
While the remnants of splendor faded away
As bright spirits sang 'mid the fields of day.

MARIA.

THE noonday sun shone hot; no dewy spot
   Remained untouched by its yellow glare:
O'er the restless sea, on the barren lea,
    And all on the flowerets fair,
It ghastly shone, while the wind made moan;
    And flying through the air
A thousand things with noisy wings,
    Which seemed, in my despair,
Like a mottled crew of spirits damned,
Or a legion that throng in Hades land.

For dead on her bier was fair Maria,
    Lying so cold and white,
Unheeding my grief, and never needing
    Throughout the day and solemn night

The ministries of love; but as the snow-white dove
    Plumes its wings, and takes its flight,
Her soul soared away where endless day
    Is never merged into dreary night.

THE BURIAL.

SLOW tramp of muffled feet;
    Slow roll of muffled drum;
Sad and slow the dirges beat
    As sad and slow they come
Winding through the crowded street,
    Under the fretted dome;

Winding upward o'er the hills,
    Downward winding through the fields,
Onward past the forest rills:
    Still the mournful music peals;
Still the tramp of muffled feet
Echoes through the sounding street;
And the muffled drum beats slow
As the dirges outward flow.

Tramp, tramp! roll, roll!
  'Tis only the dust ye bear away:
The soul has reached the shining goal
  Up in the fields of endless day.

⁓≈⁓

TO MY BELOVED DAUGHTER LILLIE.

BEAUTIFUL home in heaven away;
Beautiful angels in bright array;
Beautiful city with streets of gold;
Beautiful sea in waveless fold,
Lying amid whose silver strand,
Stretcheth adown the shining land.

Beautiful streets that wind about;
Beautiful gates that shut me out,
Wrought with pearl and starry crown
In wondrous glory sweeping down;
Beautiful shore where spirits sing
With harps of gold, and snowy wing

Plumed for flight, and mission of love.
O beautiful home in heaven above!

Strange, sweet city, that hath no night !
O glorious land beyond my sight !
I long to wander by thy silver sea ;
I wait for thy glory to shine on me.

COME UP HIGHER.

SLOWLY drifting with the tide,
  Counting all the fleeting hours ;
Aimless drifting far and wide
  Underneath the pitiless showers, —

Underneath dull, heavy clouds,
That inwrap the sky in misty shrouds,
Which sunbeam·parteth not, nor moonlight glow,
Nor shine of stars on the earth below ;

Holding in my fevered grasp
  Withered emblems of my youth ;
Gathering eagerly, as I pass,
  Emblems of unspotted truth ;

Seeing in the distance the fadeless shore ;
Hearing, far above life's din and roar,

The low, faint chant of an angel-choir,
In echoing strains, " Oh ! come up higher."

What if my bark sails slowly out
   With the sluggish, creeping tide,
Or whirls in the eddy idly about,
   Or mockingly doth ride
O'er sunken reef, on the billow's crest,
Or sweeping on in gloom and unrest?

I know that at last my weary feet
   Shall pause by the shining sea ;
I know that at last the loved I shall greet
   Who on earth were lost to me ;
While, reaching far down from their deathless land,
The long-drawn link, the invisible band,
I seem to hold in my trembling hand.

So I smile at the cloud ; I smile at the storms ;
   I smile at the pitiless showers :
On fadeless shores I discern bright forms,
   And hear, through the fleeting hours,
The low, sweet strains of the angel-choir,
Chanting ever to me, " Oh ! come up higher."

ON THE SANDS.

On the shifting sands we found her,
   On the silver sands, asleep:
The summer-winds stole around her;
   The sea rolled at her feet, —
The chainless sea, that bound her
   Unto this slumber deep.

A sunbeam kissed her raven hair,
Wondering why so cold and fair
Was the upturned marble face,
Frozen into awful grace;
Or why the fringèd eyelids lay
   Unlifted o'er the midnight eyes;
Or why the golden light of day
   Waked her not in sweet surprise.

The tide rolled out; the sullen sea
   Repeated its harsh complaint;

9

The wren piped along the fallow lea.
But there, like some blessed saint,
Undisturbed she slept: no sound,
No dreamy echoes on the hills afar,
No sunshine softly creeping round,
No gleam of evening's holiest star,
Can bid her wake,
And softly take
Along the silver sand her way,
That stretches far down to silver bay.

But the bee might strive to sip
Extracts sweet from her rigid lip;
The lapwing rest on her raven hair,
Tangling his feet,
Singing as sweet
As the angels up in mid-air;
The winds might flutter;
The fretted sea mutter,
And lament to the stones
In wild monotones:
But ever unanswering she lies
Under the glowing summer skies,
That wake her not in sweet surprise.

LYING LOW.

RAINS may beat, and winds may blow ;
The seasons come, the seasons go ;
Cold and high the winter's snow
Fall around thee, lying low ;

The richest buds of verdurous spring
    May break in beauty o'er thy grave ;
And summer suns around it cling ;
    And summer airs all lightly wave

The tasselled vines, beneath the hill
Ripple the waters by the mill,
May rustle all the waving corn ;
The smile of eve, the smile of morn,

Blush o'er the fields in bright array ;
And singing birds in forests gay
May circle and wheel above the dead ;
    Lilies white and roses red

May cast their fragrance at thy feet,
Disturbing not thy dreamless sleep:
Thy upturned face — oh ! no wind that blows
Can break its grand and calm repose.

SUMMER.

UNDER the roses the shadows lie;
On the hills the grass is green;
Down in the vale the stream rolls by,
Lit up with mystical gleam;

Across the sky the lambent folds
Of a rainbow melting away,
And mingled, fall with the sunbeam's gold
Upon the perfect fields away,

Till, as a shimmer of glory, it fadeth out, —
The shimmer not seen by mortal eyes, —
That hangeth the emerald plains about,
Stretching beyond the upper skies.

And a glow I see of all things fair —
 The purple haze of a summer's day —
Upon the fields, the sky, the air,
 And down in the vales away.

Ah! the smile of Christ is o'er all the earth,
 Till it seemeth unto me
That the glory of heaven must own its birth
 To this glory that stretches free

Around the sky, and stretches afar,
 Till, pale and sweet, it seems to hold
A radiance like a morning star
 Within its mystic fold.

MUSINGS.

ALONE I sit in this midnight hour:
 The shrill winds pipe without;
Soft and fair a fleecy shower
 Drifts through the silent night,
And drifteth high and drifteth low
 Like a shroud of spotless white.

No moon, no stars; the leaden sky
　　Lowereth heavily as my fate;
The mocking wind echoes my sigh,—
　　Too late, too late!
But the angels must hear my yearning cry
　　Beyond the golden gate.

O winds that blow! O drifting snow!
　　O leaden, leaden sky,
That hangeth heavy, that hangeth low,
　　Undeeding my desolate cry
As I gaze afar for gleam of star,
　　Or moonbeam following nigh!

My shrouded heart, my shrouded life,
　　Will not be merged in eternal gloom:
Then cease, oh! cease, your warring strife:
　　The sun must flood that blazing noon,
That will break in glory on my soul
　　Beyond its earthly tomb.

IN DARKNESS.

I WALK in darkness: never a light
Radiates my dreary night.
I walk in darkness: O Father! come
And take thy sorrowing child up home.

I'm weary of sin; I'm weary of strife;
Bereaved and desolate, I'm weary of life.
O blessed angels, floating down
With starry pinions and starry crown!

In your spotless vestments robe my soul,
As swift the tides around me roll, —
The tides of death, the tides of sin:
Oh! ope your gates, and let me in.

The earth is fair; but fairer heaven:
Longing I wait till to my soul is given
The power to soar in spotless array
Up to the gates of eternal day,

Where my Father dwells in glory and light.
Then come, blessed angels ! in robes of white,
With harps of gold, and starry crown,
And bear me up to your sinless home.

DOWN THE BRIGHT RIVER.

Down the bright river of life we are sailing,
   Approaching an unknown land evermore,
Where birds are singing, and fresh breezes blowing,
   And sweet flowers bloom on the emerald shore.

Out with the silver tide we are ever drifting,
   While over all shines the golden sun ;
With yearning hearts we are watching and waiting
   For the mystical morrow that shall never dawn.

Perchance, while we wait for its glint and gleam
   All through life's fret and its fever,
We forget, evermore, that shining shore
   To which we are all drifting ever.

MELANCHOLY.

THE long golden day has sped away
   With time in its tireless flight;
And I sit and muse in the twilight's gray,
   While its shadows deepen into night.

From out my dead past shadowy forms arise;
   While the waves of the sullen sea
Roll up at my feet, and roll and beat
   Like a long, mournful symphony.

Up from the flower-crowned hills far away
   The crescent moon in her glory has risen;
And her white beams fall on the moaning sea,
   Light as a zephyr from heaven.

From the flower-crowned hills and the moaning sea,
   From the newly-risen moon,
From the light and beauty of the earth and sky,
   Sadly and mournfully I turn:

For nevermore can summer's golden bloom
   Waken in my heart its former joy;
Nor friendship nor love, nor hope nor peace,
   'Allure me to destroy.

~≈~

AN IDYL.

BLUE is the sky, and the sunshine golden;
   Fragrant the summer-flowers;
Warble the birds in the tree-tops olden
   All through the slow, still hours;

Fresh blow the breezes, and lightly wander
   O'er the wild rose in its bloom;
From all the sunny fields the sweet white clover
   Sends forth a rich perfume.

Sounds in the distance the rush of the river
   In the hush of this summer's day:
On its glancing waves the tall willows quiver
   As it restlessly rolls away.

Pass not away, O golden hours of summer!
   Still blow, fragrant breeze!
Roll, ceaseless roll, thou never-resting river!
   Birds, still warble in waving trees!

For on the sunny hillside is sleeping my lover;
   He will waken nevermore:
So bloom, sweet flowers! and, sunshine! quiver
   The sacred spot all o'er.

NO MORE.

CRUSHED by Fate's relentless hand,
   My soul, that heavenward would soar,
Earthward takes its grovelling way,
   And echoes that sad refrain, " No more, no more! "

The wild winds that sweep o'er the desolate sea,
   And the wild waves that roll on the sandy shore,
And thunder and foam against the rock-bound coast,
   Echo ever to me mournfully, " No more, no more! "

And the tempest that rages with the angry sea,
    And the threatening clouds that lower,
And go hurrying by o'er the darkened sky,
    Seem to whisper, " No more, no more ! "

Time, that creeps with such silent step
    O'er marble column and marble floor,
' Points his shadowy hand to decay,
    And traces there, "·No more, no more ! "

GOOD-NIGHT.

My darling, my darling, a fond good-night !
God's angels keep thee till the morning light
Breaks over the headlands and over the sea,
Bringing health and hope and peace to thee.

Good-night ! Now glittering afar
In yon blue heaven, there's many a star ;
And the crescent moon sheds her golden beams
O'er thy repose and thy midnight dreams.

Sweet be that repose! and may thy dreams
Be overshadowed with glimpses and gleams
Of the river of life and the heavenly shore,
Where sorrow and pain and parting are o'er!

AT REST.

On her lonely grave how softly falls
   The shimmering light of the crescent moon,
Like a mantle of glory enshrouding the spot,
   And deepening its mystical gloom!

Morn's golden light, the blaze of noonday sun,
  . The song of birds, the busy hum of bees,
Nor rush of waters, nor wave of woods,
   Nor bloom of flowers, nor murmur of breeze,

No sound from this life and its wearying strife,
   No mortal care or pain,
No voice of love, nor voice of grief,
   Can waken to life again.

O'er the pulseless heart lie the folded hands,
  Forever, forever at rest; ·
While the mould is gathering on cheek and on brow
  Which erst our lips have pressed.

Life's pain all o'er, on yon shining shore,
  Arrayed in robes of white,
With the angel-band at God's right hand
  She walks in love and light.

WHAT THE MOON SAW.

NIGHT brooded o'er all the earth
  Like a mournful sable pall ;
The flowers slept even, and the stars
  Shone dimly over all ;
While through the shadows my vision sought
  To peer beyond the narrow wall
That girt my soul with invisible bands,
  And to hear the invisible fall
Of the footsteps of angels and the spirit-band
That come and go from the spirit-land.

Not long with triumph the darkness rode
    O'er all the silent world ;
For the moon rose up from the eastern hills,
    And swiftly and quickly hurled
Into night's abyss the great dark cloud
    That its banner had all unfurled,
And serenely sailed on with all her train,
Till her broad beams girt the mighty plain.

In all her beauty she ever looked down
    On many a hidden scene,
And never paused till her radiance fell
    And flashed with softer gleam
On the cottage low where the maiden slept,
    And kissed her in her dream ;
While she glanced on the dead that silently sleep,
No more to waken, no more to weep.

On the lake's deep bosom she saw
    An image like her own ;
And tarried there till the rippling waves
    With reflected glory shone,
And soft opaline hues, with changeful light,
    From all the starry dome ;

While the heart of the rose she softly kissed,
And stole a fragrance it never missed.

The murderer stayed his bloody hand,
　　And with fearing glances sought
To hide underneath the flowery sod
　　The ruin that he had wrought;
But the moon shone on it with terrible light,
　　Till the ghastly thing seemed fraught
With power and motion and life renewed,
Threatening him still in menacing mood.

And the moon sailed on, and sailed away,
　　And high in the heavens rode:
While the prisoner slept in his lonely cell,
　　And dreamed of summer wood
And blossoming hill and pleasant vale,
　　Where the odorous pine-tree stood;
And her silver beams fell with tender grace
Around and across his dreaming face.

And I saw her track on the mighty sea,
　　And on the rock-bound shore:
She walked the mountain, and it glowed
　　With mellow radiance o'er;

And tipped the rifting clouds, until they shone
With newer beauty all her own.

But, while she moved so calmly on,
   The whispering winds began to sigh,
And the hills looked gray; while rosy morn
   Unveiled the luminous sky,
And the god of day quenched her paler gleams
In the glory and shine of his dazzling beams.

LOST.

I BARTERED my soul for a morsel of bread, —
   There was none to cry me nay;
Ay, bartered my soul, while all my peace fled
   On that fatal, fatal day.

To-day I sit in my garnished room
   With my books and paintings rare:
But shrouded am I in sorrow and gloom;
   And Remorse, as a guest, sits there.

10

A slanting sunbeam resplendent creeps
    O'er lilies and roses combined ;
And sings my bird in his golden-wired cage,
    While sadly I weep in mine.

Waves of rich music are swelling high,
    Blent with the harp's sweeter tone ;
While my heart is making a desolate cry
    For the hours that are dead and gone.

Some day they'll shroud me in spotless white,
    The coffin-lid close o'er my breast, ·
And make me a grave 'neath the emerald turf,
    And lay me away to rest.

A DYING HYMN.

O SPIRIT waiting on the other side !
    O angel with snowy wing !
Ere I battling sink 'neath Death's cold tide,
    Let me His praises sing

Who hath led my trembling steps
   Nigh to the sacred fount,
Filled with his sacred blood ;
   And, ere to the skies I mount,

Proclaim to the amazèd world
   The glories that I behold,
Above the heavens unfurled, —
   The streets of spotless gold,

Stretched round a silver sea,
   Around the great white throne,
Where in dazzling glory dwelleth He
   Who hath all our sorrows known ;

Who ransomed our souls from death :
   Then, ere I mount to the skies,
Let His praises roll with my latest breath
   Up to the fields of paradise.

AN AUTUMN DAY.

THE glint of yellow sunshine enveloped all the har-
    vest-fields ;
  Beneath the reapers' touch the ripe grain fell ;
The wild bird trilled its song in the neighboring haw-
    thorn-tree ;
  A tiny brook twined, murmuring, through the for-
    est-dell ;

The fresh breeze swayed the silken-tasselled corn,
And wandered idly o'er the fragrant, odorous fields ;
Pausing oft to toy with the blossoming rose,
Scattering the dew-drops from its glossy leaves.

Ah, happy morn ! ah, genial summer-hours !
Perished all your brightness, faded all your bloom :
On the barren hill-top high shines the yellow sun —
Shines with ghastly splendor — till the weary day is
    done.

All my hopes are withered, as withered is your bloom;
Enshrouded are the hours in heaviness and gloom:
In all life's love and beauty my soul it hath no part;
For a grave is on the hillside, a grave is in my heart.

RAIN.

DRIP, drip, O melancholy rain!
  Through all the silent hour;
Fall, softly fall, O summer rain!
  On bud and opening flower;
On sweet wild rose and star-wort white;
On odorous pink and daisy bright;
On fresh, green grass; on clover sweet;
On tasselled corn and waving wheat;
On singing brook as it rushes by;
On lakelets deep where shadows lie;
On forest dense where the branching trees
Droop low with rain, — on their glossy leaves
Fall, softly fall, with dreary sound;
Drip, slowly drip, on the lowly mound,
Where in solemn repose we ever keep
The shrouded dead in slumbers deep.

A FRAGMENT.

FOLD lightly over him the sable pall, —
　A great soul has sought its rest;
Gently let the nerveless hands fall
　Over the pulseless breast;
Soft my mournful music swell
In dirge-like tones a solemn knell　　　.
For the departed soul, whose upward flight
Is stayed in realms of endless light.

Open wide the casement: sun and breeze
　Disturb not his sleep;
Odors faint from fragrant fields
　Softly round him creep.
Sing, bird! in yonder blackthorn-bush;
In the hedges pipe, O melancholy thrush!
Gather from the rose-tree its shining blooms,
From the nodding cypress its velvet plumes;
Crown with amaranth and myrtle his cold, white brow;
Breathe no tender token; he will not heed thee now:

Death mysterious has gathered in his fold
The casket that enshrined a soul of rarest mould.
So close the coffin-lid, and bear him slowly on,
Life's battle all fought, its victories all won.

NOWHERE TO GO.

ANGELS of mercy, angels of light,
Ranges your vision o'er this pitiful sight?
Lost, betrayed, abandoned, so low,
Angels of mercy, with nowhere to go!

Out in the night, out in the sleet,
While roll the curdled waves up at her feet;
And the home-lights glimmer, and softly throw
Pale shades on her form with nowhere to go.

Her yellow hair unbraided hangs,
While clings the dampness to every strand;
And cold and bitter the night-winds blow
Across her brow that hath nowhere to go.

A child in years, innocent and fair
As spring's sweet blossoms which perfume the air :
In her young heart was love's first glow :
Why cast her forth with nowhere to go ?

See ! — white hands are raised, and flutter aloft ;
While pale lips lisp a prayer, so low and soft,
That the angels must hear as they peer below
On her in darkness with nowhere to go.

On ear attuned to love harsh words fall ;
Out in the night strange voices call ;
While high dash the billows, and wildly flow,
As if to embrace her with nowhere to go.

Hopeless she lingers ; the lights are gone ;
While the heavy hours creep slowly on.
O angels of mercy ! around her throw
Your sinless robes, that hath nowhere to go.

Too late, too late ! the hour has passed ;
Life's sands run low ; the die is cast ;
Weird forms glide up from the depths below,
Wildly beckoning her that hath nowhere to go.

One fatal leap, the dread waves roll
Swift and high on the sandy shoal,
Undisturbing her in her sleep below,
That forth was cast with nowhere to go.

ON THE BANK OF THE PLATTE.

THE air grows mild; gentle breezes sweep
    Across the flower-gemmed plains;
While, peeping forth in emerald tufts .
    All adown the sunny lanes,
The velvet grass and shining buds
    Unfold beneath the genial rains.

And I walk on the river's strand,
    And list to the solemn waves
That roll o'er the shifting sand;
    While the silvery water laves
The banks where wild roses bloom,
And send abroad a rich perfume.

From the tops of the willow and poplar trees
  A meadow-lark trills forth its song
In bugle-notes from bank to bank,
  Which die away in echoes long ;
And all sweet sounds of hill and main
Together blend in harmonious strain.

A rainbow spans the ether blue,
  Reflecting in the shining deeps ;
While float the rifting clouds across,
  Or piled in billowy heaps
O'er the distant mount, where thunders die
Away in one long, lingering sigh.

And onward the swift river sweeps,
  Winding through sunny plains,
Down rocky chasms and craggy steeps,
  O'erleaping the glittering chains
Of mountains that sleep 'neath eternal snows,
While on, ever on, it restless flows.

Ah, beautiful river ! I liken thee
  To the struggling, waiting soul,
Whose flight must onward and upward be
  To reach the shining goal

Where the angels wait at the golden gate,
  And backward the curtain roll
That hides from our vision the jasper walls
Of the city eternal, where no night falls.

TO A STAR.

SHINE on, sweet star! shine on:
  The moon hath hid her face;
Yon angry mass that hangeth up
  Veileth her gentle grace;
The night-winds blow across the wold;
  The tide rolls on the shore;
High it beats o'er the shifting sands
  With sad and sullen roar.

One rift breaks in the clouds:
  'Tis like a sapphire band
With precious jewels studded round,
  Gleaming bright and grand.
In its midst thou art set,
  Surpassing sweet and rare, .
Brighter than gem in regal crown,
  Glistening soft and fair.

Sad is my soul, sweet star!
  The night-winds blow around:
Sweep they from the hills afar
  With low and wailing sound.
The sea is black like one vast plain,
  And at my feet doth roll,
And beat against the rocky main
  Like a spirit in its dole.

Dost pity me, pale star?
  For thou hast dimmer grown;
And angry clouds arise to mar
  The sapphire of thy throne.
Cold raindrops fall upon thy brow;
  Upon the restless sea they fall:
Blacker creep the shadows now
  Around the gray sea-wall.

Oh, shine on me, pale star!
  Until thy radiant beams
Dispel the shadows from my soul,
  The spectre from my dreams.
Farewell, sweet star! the angels now,
  That dwell in worlds of light,

Downward sweep around my brow
   Their pinions of snowy white.

For on my spirit a calm there falls,
   On the restless sea a calm ;
The winds beat about the ancient walls,
   And all their breath a balm.
A light I see at the western gate,
   That shutteth within its folds
The pearly streets, with jasper wrought,
   No mortal eye beholds.

Oh ! dim and misty is all the earth ;
   Oh ! bright and fair is heaven :
Only flowers that perish, and hollow mirth,
   Unto this life are given.
Placid the sea that stretches afar ;
   Oh ! placid the silver sea :
Beyond the gleam of sun or star,
   Oh ! bright the land which awaiteth me.

SPIRIT OF GRACE.

DESCEND, sweet spirit of grace !
　With healing balm into my soul;
And let me hide my ravished face
　While hideous waves around me roll,

And darkness and sin encompass me,
　Sorrow and one drear night :
Oh ! let me not thy mercy flee,
　Radiant spirit of light !

Oh ! guide my trembling step
　As it presses the thorny way,
Till, life's pain all o'er, its tears all wept,
　I wake in one eternal day.

THE BLOOD OF CHRIST.

AROUND me there floweth a river ;
    Its waters are black and cold :
Sweeping up in icy shiver,
    Unto my feet they fold.

Unto my garments' snowy whiteness
    The lapping tide leaps up ;
But above an angel floats in brightness,
    Holding a golden cup.

With eyes tender and merciful,
    With wings of snow, it bends down,
In garments of glory all lustreful,
    Wearing a golden crown.

From the golden cup there drippeth
    Many a crimson drop :
One into the cold river slippeth, —
    Slippeth soundless and soft.

And the black waves whiten into glory
 As high around me they swell;
While back the angel floats all swiftly
 The old sweet story to tell, —

How a soul is crossing the dark river,
 Redeemed by the Saviour's blood;
And the wide arch of heaven doth quiver
 With music that rolls like a flood.

A VISION.

THE cloudy canopy, that all day has hung
 Above the mountains craggy and old,
Floats away in purple and crimson robes
 Dyed with the sunset's gold.

On each snow-capped summit gently lingers,
 With a soft yet radiant light,
The last faint gleams of the departing day,
 Blending with the shadowy night.

Perhaps, in this mystical hour, the angels
    That dwell around the white throne
Breathe words of sweet peace and comfort
    To the soul that sorrows alone.

Methinks I hear the trail of their garments,
    And the echoes of holy strains;
See the shadowy forms of the spirit-band
    That dwells on the upper plains.

And above the white clouds I see
    What might be the jasper walls,
And the glitter and sheen of the golden streets,
    Where no night ever falls.

No more on my earth-dimmed vision
    Shall fall this radiant light,
Till the angel of death shall waft my soul
    Beyond the shades of night.

11

D A W N.

THE mist hangs o'er the mountains,
　　Transparent and light,
The distant peaks all crowning
　　With veils of fleecy white.
Above, the gray clouds are sailing,
　　Tipped with a rosy hue;
While through their deeps are peeping
　　Long belts of sunny blue;
And on the plains all glittering
　　Are drops of shining dew.
The lark's clear notes are blending
　　With the musical hum
Tiny insects forth are sending,
　　All in the brightening morn;
While gentle breezes are roaming,
　　Or playing hide-and-seek,
With the glossy leaflets toying,
　　Luring the violets meek

In an odorous couch low sleeping
    Beside the hollow rock,
Under which the streamlets gliding
    The echoes seem to mock ;
And the sweet wild rose is blooming
    Beside the waxen gem
That into glad life is springing
    In many a hidden glen ;
And a radiant beauty is shrouding
    The earth and sunny sky,
Like the far and faintest echo
    Of music floating by.
Then we sit in the mystic gloaming,
    And list for the spirit-band
That on heavenly plains are watching,
    And wait on the golden strand
For the soul that is slowly passing
    On to their brighter land.

NORA.

ONCE I passed a village sweet:
Purple hills intwined its feet;
A river bound it with one great stride.
As, lo! I paused in the summer-tide,
Thinking, perchance, some angel-eyes
Might glance down from paradise
Upon this spot, glowing that day
Among the massive hills away,
Strolling down a mossy lane,
Sweet with pansy and golden-fane,
The glory of earth, the glory of sky,
Seemed a reflex to my longing eye
Of that greater glory up on high.
Then plaintive strains I loved to hear
Of olden music broke on mine ear,
Joining my voice to the old-time song,
Singing, methought, with an angel-throng,
Till I remembered a day in the long-ago
When I walked these fields with heart aglow.

I sang to the skies; I sang to the trees;
Crooned I low to the crooning breeze:
Singing, I said, " O nestling town,
Wearing summer's purple crown !
I hear your brisk and busy hum ;
I see your shadows go and come ;
And softly well your noontide bells
Under the sounding echoes swells,
Clear and low, soft and slow ;
Outward flaunt your chimings low ;
While upward creeps the golden glow
Of the noontide sun from the vale below ;
And, echoing through the sounding street,
Lo ! the hurrying footsteps meet.
From the church's steeple tall
The ring-necked pigeon's cooing call
Is answered from the mossy caves
Where the twining ivy cleaves,
And in quaint and antique lines
All the mouldering pile enshrines.
Just above, the roses blow
In robes as white as the living snow ;
Just above, the violets sweet
Hide their clusters at my feet,

With their odors faint and rare
Scenting all the balmy air;
Just above, the churchyard lies,
Where straight the gleaming shafts arise
Straight and tall to the glowing skies;
Round, round, the river whirls,
Swift and deep, in eddying curls,
Silvering the banks with silver pearls·
As it beats and moans in sounding tones,
Breaking soft its flecking foams
Against the gray and mossy stones,
Till in calmness its crystal water meets
A lake that all unrippled sleeps
Amid the shadows long and gray,
Clasped around the radiant day."

Afloat on its surface, in fine array
And in bridal vesture, the lilies lay;
While down from the heavens the roving sun
Kissed their bright petals one by one;
While music of lapwing and drowsy bee
Stole like the whir of a distant sea;
And rose the sound of the sobbing pine
In the noontide air like a sobbing chime,

And, as censer swung the fields among,
Their spicy fragrance far outward flung.
And on this day, hand in hand,
Two walked up the emerald strand, —
By the river walked, and under the pines,
That never stilled their sobbing chimes;
And by the lake where the lilies white
Uplifted lay in the golden light,
And the wild convolvulus in clusters twines
Its purple bells on purple vines.
Oh! Nora was fair; oh! Nora was sweet
As the purple glorias at her feet.
But Nora was proud, Nora was cold,
To all that wooed not with their gold.
The lilies she twisted into a crown;
In silken threads her hair hung down, —
Black it hung as the raven's wing,
Silky and soft as the wild lapwing.
The lilies she twined around her brow,
And tossed the floss about her now, —
The floss that stole the purple gleam,
The softer glory of a sunbeam;
Her eyes that shone as worlds of light
Might on this at wan midnight;

Luminous and deep as pool asleep
When over the sun pale shadows creep;
Liquid and soft as the stars up aloft,
That midnight vigils keep;
Graceful as the bending willow,
Pliant as the heaving billow,
Stately, with a winning grace,
As if her soul indexed her face;
Pleasant her mien, and with all blent
Was courteous, sweet, and kind, content
That heaven vouchsafèd such a friend
Whose soul in harmony could blend
With hers in the gold of summer-tide.
'And " Ah, 'tis sweet ! " she faintly sighed;
But all the while she wished away
The luckless wight that came that day.
White his brow and broad;
Stately his step as he firmly trod
Under his feet the grasses sweet, —
Under his feet as by her side
He walked in the golden summer-tide.
He plucked the lilies, the purple vines,
And needles sharp from the velvet pines,
And pinned them into the wild bluebells
Clustering in the shady dells.

And passionate his tones, and deep
As the summer-winds that seek
The deepest labyrinths of a cave
Winding 'neath the ocean's wave.
Said he, " Nora, my love, the stars above,
    That constant vigils keep;
The moon that sails like a white-winged dove
    Up through the amber deep,
And saileth east, and saileth west,
    O'er all the world asleep;
The roving sun in yonder sky,
    That gilds the morn, that gilds the eve;
The river that sweeps all swiftly by;
    The ivy intwining the mossy eaves;
The tide that rolls out, the tide that rolls in
From the swelling sea in unceasing din,
Day unto day, night unto night;
The seasons, unfolding their robes of light, —
Are not more constant, O Nora sweet!
Than thy lover kneeling at thy feet.
Wealth I have none, but a strong right arm
That will be thy shield in life's alarm,
And a heart that's brave in its love for thee.
O Nora! look up and answer me."

Pale Nora grew: the lapwing flew,
And screeched out a dismal note;
The sweet sun, smote by a cloud afloat,
  Hid in its thick and fleecy fold;
The river swept on to a sunless moat;
  The daisies closed up their eyes of gold.
Oh! scornful she grew; and wildly flew
  The lapwing up to the cloud;
The wind it blew through the sobbing yew
  In 'plaining sad and loud;
And unto the feet of Nora sweet, —
  Nora the rare and proud.
One moment shone in her midnight eyes
  A look of love such as angels wear;
Then scorn, contempt, and cold surprise,
  Came from Nora the proud and rare.
" Go, base-born! from my sight retire!
Nor strike for me love's ardent lyre.
See these gems that grace my silk attire!
They burn and sparkle with living fire:
  Canst bring them to me from over the sea?
If not," she cried, " retire! "
Then white he grew as a winding-sheet
Wrapping the dead in eternal sleep.

All anguished his looks, but haughty his step,
  As he strode with firmness over the fields,
As a ship that rides one moment erect
  Before to the tide she yields;
And the sounding swell of the noontide bell
· Had hushed its clanging peal;
And Nora had torn the lily crown
From the silken threads hanging adown,
  As from the heart she tore the part
That should have been its lily crown.
He fled to distant lands, and sought
The wealth that with it honors brought;
But ever saw a snow-white hand
Plucking lilies from flossy band;
The look of scorn, contempt, surprise,
Flashing from her midnight eyes;
And the decayed and mossy eaves
Where the twining ivy cleaves;
Heard the sounding peal
Of a bell across the field,
And the river's gladsome whirls
Casting forth the silver pearls.
" Oh bitter remembrance! O Nora proud!
  Ever my heart must beat for thee,

Till at last I shall sleep in my winding-sheet
  Alone by the desolate sea!"
Thus he cried to the mocking tide
  That ploughed the furrowed lea.
The dazzled world at her proud shrine
  Bowed its adoring head,
And seasons rolled into summer prime;
  But Nora remained unwed.
Her silken hair was fading out,
  From her midnight orbs the light;
The bloom on her cheek Time put to rout,
  And yellowed its marble white;
But stately her step with stately grace,
And proud the look that indexed her face
As she saw the lilies, the purple bells,
Clustering down in the forest-dells,
And heard the ring-necked pigeon's call
From the church's steeple tall,
And walked the fields in the summer-tide
That the river bound with one great stride.
But, alone in her pride, alone she sighed
  Unto the blossoming flower.
The lapwing heard, and her espied
  Up in his windy tower,

And shrieking flew from the sobbing yew
   Unto a sunnier bower.
For Nora the fair, Nora the rare,
   Wept for her lover lost :
Dead leaves she plucked, saying, " I'll wear
   Among the folds of my silken floss
These withered emblems everywhere."
She plucked from her bosom the rarest pearls,
And flung them into the eddying curls
   Of the river that hid them deep amid
The fold and curl of its restless whirls,
   Crying, " Woe is me ! over the sea
   My lover sailed away.
Now dimmed the stars, the moonbeams paled,
   And the glowing fields of May.
I see through a mist, that might, I wist,
   As I sing my mournful lay,
Blind mine eyes to the radiant skies,
   The gold of a summer-day.
I'll seek my lover where the white sea-plover
   Pipeth unto the marsh ;
Where sips the bee from the honeyed clover,
   And the raven croaketh harsh."

She wandered east, she wandered west,
    O'er many a vine-clad shore,
That soothèd not her heart's unrest,
    Beating to the measures of " Nevermore ; "
Till a city she gained, old and quaint,
With temples upreared to some holy saint ;
    And the sea it rolled round the city old,
E'en to the feet of the ancient streets
Swept it up like glittering sheets,
And its sounding tide far and wide
    Furrowed the fallow lea ;
And the lover she wept, lo ! there he slept
    Alone by the desolate sea.

PARTED.

SOFT shone the southern sun ;
    Blue shone the sky ;
Slow flitting, one by one,
    The golden hours went by.

Low we bowed before the altar,
　As priest in stole of white
Said, " Until death doth sever,
　I these two unite."

But one day we parted, —
　One sunny summer day :
Now I wander broken-hearted
　In the shadows alway.

That was long ago ; but never
　Shall we meet again
Under the blue sky, never
　Under the rain.

And I linger in the even
　When the pale stars shine,
Looking upward to heaven,
　Beyond change or time,

Thinking of a greeting
　All on its blessed shore ;
Thinking of a meeting
　Where parting is no more.

DEAD.

How cold and still where late the life-blood
Surged through the veins in crimson tide!
How pulseless the heart that beat with ambition
And high hopes, and fluttered at the coming
Of my footstep o'er the emerald sward!
On the brow where gentle graces thronèd sat,
There is no mark left by the soul that struggled
For release from its mysterious tenement,
But a smile, that the angels who wafted
Thy pure spirit up to heavenly plains
Might envy. Thy golden hair, that, unconfined,
Sweeps down in shining folds across thy marbled neck,
And o'er thy spotless shroud, lying like
Rippling waves all on thy bier, is softly stirred
By the fragrant winds that creep through
The open casement. The earth its fairest aspect wears,
As if to mock thee lying there so cold and still.

Outside, the red-winged oriole flaunts his plumage gay,
And soars into the blue deep, trilling his sweetest song ;
While the oleander blossoms in the hawthorn shade.
The timid fawn, thy pet and plaything,
Retires not now at my approach,
But watches with its great beseeching eyes
For the coming of thy footsteps down the garden-walk.
The busy world keeps up its masquerade and farce,
Where hearts are broken, and souls bartered
For that glittering dross that men call gold.
Through the sunny summer-fields I walk as in a dream,
Crushing the purple daisies 'neath my feet, mindful
    only
Of the hours when I plucked them for thy pleasure.
The skiff lies moored within the shadow
Of the ancient pine that overhangs the banks
Of the lake whose glittering surface
Erst was rippled by the course it made
When freighted by our happy hearts.
Thou wert the secret link that bound my soul
Unto a higher life, which is not broken,
But drawn out in greater lengths, that reach
Even now from thine eternal home
Down to me stricken and dazed with grief.

And I must see the casket that enshrined
So fair a jewel borne from me,
And shrouded 'neath the damp and mould ;
While I forevermore shall go through life
Inwrapped with pain and grief
That death hath severed this my earthly bond.
No voice of mine crying up to God
Can call thee back, that art among the angels ;
And so my soul yearns for gentle patience
To infold me like a white-winged dove,
Until I, too, shall shrouded sleep,
And summer-winds a requiem keep,
And daisies bloom, and forest-flowers,
And genial sun, and gentle showers,
Fall on my grave through the summer-hours.

THE MORNING-GLORY.

ONE day I sat within my room,
　　All sick, and bowed with grief:
The sound of rain fell on my heart
　　As drops on the withered leaf;
And the winds made moan, and the winds made sigh,
Like a human heart in its desolate cry:
It beat at the pane, with the raindrops beat,
And stole like a wail round the dead in their sleep.

The sky was heavy, the sky was gray;
　　And darkly lowered the clouds:
They shut out the sunshine, they shut out the blue,
　　And hung o'er the mountains in watery shrouds,
And clung to the hills, and clung to the river,
And dropped their mists where the aspens quiver;
They bent o'er the plains, and shut from my view
The nodding harebells purple and blue.

Alone in my grief with the mournful winds,
 And the drip, the drip, of the mournful rain,
And the shrouding mists, that shut me out
 From view of mountain, or view of plain.

'Neath my casement one flower bloomed alone :
 On it the tempest had beaten, and the falling rain ;
But it brightly bloomed and brightly shone
 As the nodding bluebells on the plain.

Its tints were pale, at the petals pale,
 But deepened into royal purple,
With the faintest pink on its delicate edge,
 And creeping round its velvet circle.

'Mid the winds that beat, and the rains that fell,
 All day it bloomed in sweetness,
And shone like a star through the desolate hours,
 And drooped its head in meekness,

Till the storm passed away, and one sunbeam
 Tarried on the hills alone,
And the rosy clouds in rosy mass
 Above the mountains shone.

One parting glance, its velvet folds
    Beneath the pale, the petals pale :
It bloomed no more, but shrank to death
    Underneath a leafy veil.

But I saw a moral in its brief, bright life,
    And in its pleasant ending,
And prayed that my dreary day be fraught
    With goodness and virtue, blending
With a hopeful trust through its perilous way,
That at last shall end in eternal day.

CHANGES.

A MILLION stars hung in the sky ;
    A million flowers bloomed on the earth ;
A thousand voices went whispering by ;
    A thousand souls struggled into birth.

Thousands lay dead on the battle-field ;
    Thousands languished on beds of pain ;
A thousand souls went out in the night,
    As millions swelled on the upper plain.

A million woes struck a million hearts:
　　O God! in the dank and cheerless night
A million's honor was sold in the marts,
　　As millions struggled towards the light.

A million changes rang round the world;
　　The sea rolled over its million graves,
And from its bosom, threatening, hurled
　　A million surging, seething waves.

O God! in the night raise a million souls,
　　Passing away o'er the soundless tide,
Sinking in quicksands, sinking in shoals,
　　That stretcheth 'neath them far and wide, —

O Father of mercy! raise them high, —
　　High to the land 'bove the starry dome;
And, ye guardian angels wandering nigh,
　　Oh! bear these million spirits home.

IN VAIN.

In vain for me the earth is bright;
　In vain for me the soft sunbeam
Sheds on the earth a golden light;
　In vain for me its palest gleam;

In vain, in vain, the cool wind sweeps
　Across the ancient wold;
In vain for me the moonbeam sleeps
　In faint and shadowy fold;

Oh! all in vain the roses bloom
　Within my garden-bower:
For white and cold through the misty gloom
　Cometh to me the hour

When I saw her dead.　The rosy Morn
　Her banner hung across the sky:
Its folds were crimson, and wrought upon
　With amber and purple dye.

Silent she lay in her snowy shroud;
   Upon her lip a smile:
'Twas like a moonbeam hid in cloud,
   But shining all the while.

The cloud was death: oh! nevermore
   By yonder restless sea;
Ah! nevermore, when the moonbeams pour
   Their silver flood on me,—

Shall I pause to pluck the sea-flower white,
   Lured by the creeping tide,
Or watch with her the gleaming light
   Upon the ocean ride.

O sea! dreamless within the sound
   Of thy melancholy sweeping plaint
She sleepeth now, inwrapped around
   With memories like a saint.

But now on thy shores, oh! not in vain
   Does the sunbeam gild the cloud:
Swell, restless sea! thy high refrain
   Like an anthem deep and loud.

For behold yon setting sun !
　Behold yon western sky,
With its crimson glory, sweeping down
　Where the purple masses lie !

Behind it a city there lies :
　In its midst she dwelleth now,
With a daze of glory in her eyes,
　A crown upon her brow.

She heareth me not, she seeth me not,
　As she walks by the silver sea :
Her robes are white, all lustrously wrought;
　And their lustre falls on me.

Methinks her sweet music rings
　High through the arch of heaven :
Faint echoes of the song she sings
　Steal through the gates of even.

O pearly gates that shut me out !
　O wonderful streets of gold !
O placid sea that winds about
　In many a shining fold !

I would that I dwelt within your light,
In the midst of the city fair
That stretcheth so far beyond my sight;
And she awaiteth me there.

THY WILL BE DONE.

Low unto thy will I seek to bow,
Father, dwelling up in heaven;
Though sorrows encompass me now,
As I walk through the mists of even.

Yet my soul fain would wander
Up to thy realms of light,
As all desolate I ponder.
Through my life's dreary night,

Waiting for an eternal dawning
To break upon the fields of day,
Where night is never, nor morning,
Up in the heavens away.

COME BACK.

COME back to me, O lost, lost hope !
  How the night-winds moan on the desolate shore !
Oh ! come back to me, my faith and trust ;
  Or have ye fled me forevermore ?
My frail bark lies stranded on the sluggish tide,
  Its sails all rent by the reckless storm ;
And shadowy hands are beckoning me :
  I cannot wait for the coming morn.
The heavens are black with portentous clouds :
  I know that behind them the stars still shine ;
But through their dread darkness there gleams no
      light
  Into this desolate heart of mine.

A THUNDER-STORM.

THE clouds are piled in the western sky
   Like the mountains' rugged rifts;
While the deepening thunder rolls
   Adown the rocky cliffs;
And hills repeat the echoes low
Till they die away on the plains below.

Athwart the sky, athwart the clouds,
   The lightnings zigzag flash .
Like angry bolts from heaven sent;
   And I list to the awful crash,
And tumble and roll into chasms deep,
Of rocks that are rent from the mountain steep.

The forest monarch uprooted lies,
   Of all its glory shorn;
The tempest hurls with resistless force
   The mighty flood adown

The river's bed, whose angry surge
Rises high above the storm's own dirge.

But my soul soars aloft above the din
   To the peaceful, distant shore
Where the angels wait to let me in,
   And wait and wait evermore,
With raiment white, and harps of gold,
Singing a song that is never old.

ROSES.

Roses red, roses white,
Gather for the bride to-night:
Cast them loving at her feet,
Roses red and roses sweet.

Roses red, roses white,
Gather for the dead to-night:
Bind them to the frozen feet,
Roses red and roses sweet.

Let the snowy clusters twine ;
Let the glowing red enshrine
The marble pallor of the face :
Lift the hands with gentle grace,
Folded in unbroken rest
O'er the cold and pulseless breast.

Pluck the fragrant buds of May,
Violets sweet and tulips gay ;
While the flooding light of day
Dies upon the hills away.

Roses red and roses white
Gather for the bride to-night :
Let the fragrant buds intwine,
Let the lily-blooms enshrine,
The midnight hair, the brow of snow :
The roses red her cheeks outglow.

Oh ! roses red and roses white
Gather for the dead to-night :
Let the waxen hands infold
The daisies' smile, the lilies' gold.

Wed the bride, bury the dead,
Roses white and roses red !
They will wither, they will bloom,
While foldeth the dreary night in gloom
Over the bride and over the tomb.

THOU DIDST FORGET.

ALAS! thou didst forget
   That day long ago
When under the limes we met,
   Beneath the fervid glow
Of Orient skies, and by the sea :
Thou didst forget, — ah, me !

Thy cheek was like the rose ;
   Thy midnight hair hung down ;
White lilies clasped it close,
   And wreathed it like a crown.
Thy hand that lay in mine, love,
Fluttered like a prisoned dove.

The sea it rolled away
 With many a tuneful plaint;
Soft the moonlight lay,
 Like robe upon a saint,

Over the limes. Ah me
 That thou didst forget
Under Orient skies and by the sea!
 I would we'd never met!

. . . .

You taught me to forget.

Under the limes we walked,
 Under the limes.
The wind it frisked, and mocked
 The river's chimes:
I heard it on the hills afar,
Above where gleamed the evening star.

Oh! happy was my heart that night
 Under the limes;
The moonbeams quivered white
 Under the limes;
Down in the fields the corn was ripe;
Across the meadows the call of the snipe

I heard.   The distant swell,
  The soft, mysterious chimes,
Of the winds adown the dell,
  Walking under. the limes,
And the subtle essence of many blooms
Yielding all their rich perfumes,

Came to my senses, — ah me,
  ˙ The silver chimes
Of the river and the sea,
  Under the limes !
But I would we'd never met !
For you taught me to forget

The sweetest dream of all my youth
  Under the limes :
My belief in goodness, truth,
  Listening to the chimes
Of the river and the sea,
You taught me to forget, — ah me !

13

THE WATCH-TOWER.

THE 'wildering gleams of her midnight hair
  Were hanging unto her feet
As with agile step she clomb the stair
  Her mid-day tryst to keep:
The sun hung high, and his reddening glare
Purpled the strands of her midnight hair.

The woods were aflame with red and gold;
  The ripened harvest clung
O'er the russet fields in many a fold;
  And the ripened berries hung
And hid in clusters 'mong the brown,
The red-brown leaves a-drooping down.

The great salt sea that never sleeps,
  It lay like a glassy plain;
It curled round the rocks that rose in heaps
  High 'gainst the sandy main;

Its dash and swell came like a knell, —
The distant knell of a tolling bell.

The tower was round and iron-bound,
  And fettered with gyves of steel:
A climbing rose with clusters crowned
  The gyves of iron and steel,
As the stair she clomb in breathless haste,
Scanning the salt sea's glassy waste.

And the red sun shone as a snowy sail
  She descried in the distance afar:
Her blushing cheek told its own love-tale;
  Her eyes, like the morning star,
Seemed the distance to pierce; and her raven hair
Fell at her feet as she clomb the stair.

The topmost point of the tower she reached:
  Her garments were like the snow
When it drifted lies in billowy heaps
  Beneath the moon's pale glow;
The breeze it tossed and twisted the floss,
And fanned the blush her cheek across.

On came the ship in track of foam ;
   While leaped the.dolphin high :
The salt sea looked as if newly sown
   With belts of sapphire sky.
O'er russet fields a dove she hailed
As the ship sailed on, and faster sailed.

The dove wheeled down where the roses crowned
   The gyves of iron and steel :
Around his throat she softly bound
   A tiny silken reel
All woven and wound with her midnight hair,
That reached her feet as she clomb the stair.

Up the bird floated, — up, — till a cloud
   Blackened the great salt sea ;
And the furious tide rolled like a shroud
   All over the sandy lea ;
The tower it rocked ; the wind made talk
With the waves that answered with a mock.

And round the tower the sea-bird flew ;
   The ship it sailed on ;
The wind it raved and wildly blew,
   And shrieked to the rising storm ;

The great ocean hissed and roared and foamed
Around the tower that creaked and groaned.

Her midnight hair was wet with spray;
   Her snow-white garments too:
But still the ship it sailed away,
   And the wind it blew and blew,
And the black clouds bent with withering frown,
And the red leaves fell with the russet brown;

And the tide it whirled, and the tide it curled.
   But the lady in the tower,
That clomb the stair with midnight hair
   Clasped with the running flower,
She saw the ship; its sails were rent:
She saw the dove; its strength was spent.

She heard the breakers; she heard the roar
   Around the mountains in the sea;
She saw the tide plough the sandy shore,
   And furrow the sandy lea:
The uprooted trees it quick gulped down;
While the sky looked on with withering frown,

And poured its flood, and shot out its fire,
 And rolled its thunder over the strand,
And rose and fell with fitful ire
 In vengeful mood all round the land.
The ship it plunged on like a huge bird shorn,
With broken spars and white sails gone.

On the ocean a speck, that might be a gull,
 Or a mermaid combing her hair.
Not a sound was heard 'mid the ominous lull
 That fell on the earth and air,
Till the black tower swayed, and the gyves of steel
Bent to the blast like a bending reel.

God save our souls! the ship it is doomed;
 And ocean-spirits wait
To fold beneath a sunless tomb,
 And glut and fatten and sate,
And sport with the ship as it goeth down,
While the skies look on with withering frown.

The timbers part with a creak and groan;
 Wildly the sea-spirits call;
The speck it rideth 'mid the white foam
 That riseth like a wall

Around the breakers, and round them it flies
'Mid bolts that rend the frowning skies.

Oh the tiny boat! it breasteth the storm:
   It must be an angel bright
Sits at the helm, guiding it on,
   With face like the morning light!
No: 'tis the maiden fair with midnight hair,
With garments of snow, that clomb the stair.

With a shriek and a moan the ship goes down;
   Loud the breakers roar.
Atop of the billows, atop of the foam
   That sweeps from the inland shore,
The white maid sits: her hair it dips
In the salt sea-foam that from it drips.

To a broken spar 'mid the white sea's surge
   There clingeth a manly form;
While beat and roll like a terrible dirge
   Weird spirits of the storm,
And swell and call, and call and swell, ·
And beat and beat, like a tolling bell.

But over the swell, the surge and swell,
　The small craft rideth fast:
Lo! now there pealeth the watch-tower bell;
　And its brazen tongue doth cast
All over the sea a brazen sound,
Rocking the tower with iron bound.

Steady at helm! while the merciless sea,
　Striving with might and main,
Tearing and roaring in maddest glee,
　Shrieketh out in its maddest pain:
Ah! a hand it flutters; pale lips mutter
A name alone the waves ne'er utter.

And the fluttering hand drags the stiffened form:
　Oh, the tiny boat rides fast!
Down from the tower and through the storm
　The brazen bell doth cast
Its brazen sound all over the land;
And the sea ploughs up the ancient strand.

Saved, O God! by a brave, true soul!
　An angel guided it on!
Now down from the tower there oft doth roll
　The sound of the maiden's song;

And the roses twine, and the red sunshine
Flashes soft on the ocean's brine,
Purpling the strands of her raven hair
As with agile step she climbs the stair.

A MIDNIGHT DREAM.

In my midnight dreams methought again I trod
The pleasant paths where my childish feet so oft had
strayed.
Again I wandered by the placid lake where all day
long
The birds wheeled and circled, and carolled forth
Their sweetest songs; and where the mighty forest-
trees,
Whose waving tops my vision scarce could scan,
Mirrored themselves; while through their glossy foli-
age
Long, slanting sunbeams resplendent crept.
Again for me the wild rose bloomed
With a sweetness no other roses ever had;
Again the purple violet and clover-blooms

With careless hand I plucked : and in my dream
I heard the sound of bells stealing soft upon the morn-
　　ing air ;
And, as my wont, my way I wended
To the little church where the pastor of the flock
In simple language told of One who died
To save an erring world.
Behind the church reposed in death's long sleep
My ancestors, — those who, with bold, undaunted
　　front,
Quailed not at danger, but who, with deathless
　　faith
In God, the mighty ocean crossed,
That they might worship him in peace.
Ah, heroes and conquerors in Life's fierce battle !
Are ye not angels now, where before the throne in
　　heaven
Ye worship Him both day and night ?
Still I dreamed on, and fancied in my dreams
That father, mother, sister, brother, all were there ;
And, as of old, — with smiles and gentle words,
And tones of love, that so beguile
Our youthful hearts, — with me
They still pursued life's journey, pausing oft

To pluck the sweetness from its flowers,
Lingering longest where the sunshine lingered.

Ah me! I awoke. Was it but a dream,
    That in the still night the God of all love
Sent an angel to cheer me, and bid me look
    From this sorrowful life to his mansions above?

DECORATION-DAY.

WE mourn a nation's dead to-day, —
    A nation's dead:
O Father in heaven away!
    Around us spread
A mantle of peace, till, like a sea,
Our souls unite in praise to thee.

With the sweetest blooms.of May,
    Clusters of roses red
We'll softly wreathe to-day
    Over our nation's dead;
While the muffled sound of the rolling drum
Mingling falls with the booming gun.

O'er these sacred mounds let an anthem swell
  For the nation's dead,
Till the echoes roll o'er hill and dell,
  And earth and sky seem wed,
And one grand anthem break o'er the sea,
Till worlds unite in praise to Thee.

DECORATION-HYMN.

ROUND the graves of these heroes in spotless glory
  We'll lovingly twine Spring's brightest bloom:
The infant, the youth, the aged and hoary,
  Slow passing on to the wide-yawning tomb,

Singing praises to God that peace it now floweth,
  Like a white, spotless sea, all over the land;
Till far through the wide arch of heaven it pealeth,
  And the echoing strains reach the angel-band.

In the tomb slept our Saviour: now, the Holy of ho-
    lies,
  At the right hand of God he sits on the throne,
And lovingly bends from his radiant glories
  To whisper to mortals, "Your sorrows I've known."

Scatter blossoms, sing praises ; for Jesus in heaven
  Received their bright spirits as they left the cold clay,
And swift exit made through the dim gates of even
  Up to fair fields of light beyond earth away.

THE VOICE OF NIGHT.

THE sweetest buds of May
  Shine on the fields ;
The glowing light of day
  Unto night yields.

The moon she riseth now
  Up from the eastern sea :
With faint, placid glow
  Her beams fall on me.

The stars, like gems of light,
  Glitter far away :
Out in the solemn night
  Voices seem to say, —.

Chanting to the hills
  Around the ancient sea,
Chanting to the fields
  Beyond the emerald lea, —

" There is a land of beauty,
  There is a world so bright,
Where spirits dwell in glory
  Beyond mortal sight.

" The bending heavens hide it;
  The soft, glimmering moon
Holds not a radiance like it, —
  Brighter than sun at noon."

Now the night grows dark and deeper;
  The sea wails aloud:
Pale the midnight sleeper
  Rises in his shroud;

For he hears Death a-calling;
  Beholds a spectre pale
Out of the blackness rising,
  Out of the shadowy vale;

And the angels ever chanting,
   Floating o'er the fields, —
Chanting to the darkness,
   Waiting till the peals

Of echoing music break
   Over the plains above,
And all the earth it wake
   To joy and light and love.

And on the dead and living
   The risen sun shines ;
But the angels, ever chanting
   Up in holy climes,

Wave their snowy pinions,
   And tune their harps of gold ;
And the living weep, while the dead are asleep
   Under the damp and mould.

IN THE LONG–AGO.

Soft gleamed the evening star
  In yon blue dome ;
Sailed the white moon afar,
  And on the sea shone ;
High rolled the tide, high on the shore,
And beat on the sands with sullen roar.

On the hillside the purple daisies slept,
  And slept the pale sea-flower ;
Wan the lilies looked, as if they wept
  All in night's still hour ;
Gently sighed the winds across the lone wold,
Where rested the moonbeam in shadowy fold.

On the sands we paused, then parted evermore :
  Now I wander by the gray sea alone.
The tide rolls high on the sandy shore ;
  The white moon sails through yon blue dome, —
On the lonely wold soft rest her beams ;
'Neath the boiling flood the sea-flower gleams.

But the sweet star of eve it shines not for me,
Nor soft creeps the wind across the lone lea:
But a ship I discern far out on the sea;
It sails o'er the breakers like a white-plumèd bird;
It passes the sand-bar like a spectre unheard.
Death sits at the helm, moveless and grim:
Undaunted I'll enter to welcome him.

UPON THE HEIGHTS.

Upon hoary heights I stand:
  Below me winds a stream;
Swift and broad and grand
  Its silver waters gleam
Amid plains ancient and gray,
With beauty girt this wondrous day.

Wide yawns the chasm at my feet:
  The river sweeps below;
Yet shadows soft from yonder peak,
  And the sunbeam's golden glow,
Upon it rest; while far and faint
The winds take up its echoing plaint.

14

A crimson cloud goes floating by,
   Veiling eternal snows ;
Like sapphire sea is yonder sky,
   In placid, deep repose ;
Above me far is a dove afloat,
With spotted wing and snowy throat.

The sunbeam calleth forth the flower ;
   And it lifts its beauteous head
Up to the clouds that gently lower
   White crystals round its bed,
So sweet and fair, as if angel bright
Had dropped them in its upward flight.

THE SIERRAS.

GRAND, mysterious, and sublime,
Unto the skies they towering rise ;
Unto the plains that sleep beneath
The radiant glory of a noonday sun.
A thousand lights upon them quiver ;
A thousand mystic hues inwrap them.
One peak lies all asleep

Beneath a royal-purple veil
Which lightly rests upon its hoary head
Like a regal-purple crown,
White, glittering white in massive grandeur :
Some mingle with the clouds,
Or shoot upward far beyond
All mortal ken, where sapphire
Fields above them bend, or
A sapphire waveless sea sweeps
Round them all its radiant flood.
Thought that wanders free —
The soul, the immortal soul of man —
Shrinks back in wonder at all the
Mysteries that enshroud them where they lie
Silent, save with all the voiceless things of
Nature ; silent, save when in thunder-tones
God speaks, and sends a mountain toppling
To the sea ; silent, save when an earthquake,
With one convulsive heave, rends in twain
The lofty peaks, and tears from the mountain's
Heart its secrets, revealing to the
Astonished gaze chambers peopled
With a thousand mysteries, as if
Worlds had gone to sleep, and froze.

DOLOR.

MORN flushed the sky; the sun
   Rose radiant o'er the fields of day;
The dun-hued shadows melted one by one
   Into unknown realms away.

I walked abroad: in globules bright
   Upon the grass the dew-drops lay;
Upon the fields the star-blooms white
   Unfolded 'neath the sun's soft ray;
      And stole around
      The low, faint sound
Of the whispering winds at play.
   To stately heights, and snowy-crowned,
The mountains uprose in the distance away,
      And brave and grand
      In this summer-land,
Stretching far out in bold array;

And the bending skies
In sweet surprise
Blushed till their sapphire hues
Wore rosy crown that softly shone
Like a halo bright on the misty white,
On the fields aglow with purple light.

Oh ! never shone a fairer morn
Than this morn that shone on me :
Birds ne'er warbled a sweeter song
Than my heart in its joy and glee.

But an hour passed by : athwart the sky
Circled a cold, gray cloud ;
The wind died out with a wail and a sigh ;
The mountains were hid in a misty shroud :

And my joy went out with the soft sunshine ;
With the frowning clouds it fled :
Now ghastly and pale these hands of mine
Close round it cold and dead.

TO JOSEPHINE.

THE night has fled; sweet morn
  Has wakened all the earth anew;
Grand, fair, serene, the rising sun
  Climbs up a sea of blue,
And smiles.   Forthwith the smiling sky
Is all ablaze.   The mountains blush.
Yon peak, folded 'neath eternal snows,
Has donned a royal-purple robe
Befitting kings.
The modest hills blush too.
The ancient plains lie wrapped
In splendor, like a sea of gold.
Each withered blade of grass
Might be a silver spear
Dotted with diamonds.
Worlds wake up: alas for me!
I wake to sorrow; while from

Life's poisoned chalice I turn
In bitterness away.   Out upon
Its troubled sea my frail bark
Drifts and drifts on to unknown shores :
Beneath my feet the billows heave,
And all the trembling flood sweeps
Round me like an icy shroud.
Afar, only afar, I see the spotless
Glory of a day lit up with gladness ;
Cool winds fan my fevered brow ;
The hum of life begins ;
And ships go by with sails
Unfurled, like bird on snowy wing.
Alas ! life's mocking sea
Tempts me to end all weariness
In this unwearying strife, and bid
Farewell to earth and sky,
And make this glorious sun a shroud
Wherewith to wrap my weary
Feet around ; this radiant earth
A pillow, whereon I may repose
In dreamless slumber evermore,
That tender voice of child
Or friend calling through

The gloom I should not hear,
Nor hear the singing birds,
Nor see glad spring break on
The world once more.
Ah, death comes not for me !
Life is the crucible wherein
My soul awaits its purifying.
That process o'er, these griefs will fade ;
These pains that now convulse my soul
Will be but earthly shadows
Scattered 'mid the waste of time.
Eternity's vast shores loom on my vision,
Grander, fairer than the sun,
More glorious than the day begun ;
And my tired spirit patient waits
For angels to fold the golden gates
Back for my entrance into worlds of light
Beyond the change of day or night.